"It's going to be an advice column," Luke said. "You're going to write it."

"I'm not sure I could. It sounds tricky," Sam said.

"You'd be perfect for it. You're patient, you're sympathetic, you understand people."

Sam had the uncomfortable feeling she was being buttered up again, but when she analyzed what Luke had said word by word, she had to admit that it was true.

"More important," he added. "You don't have a distinctive writing style. You see, nobody is going to know that you're writing it. If they know it's only you, they won't have any respect for the column."

"Thanks a lot!"

"I didn't mean that! All I mean is that nobody takes anything seriously when they know that whoever is doing it is just another junior at Lee High. Complete anonymity is basic. I've got it all figured out."

Later on, looking back, Sam could not remember exactly agreeing to the plan. In fact, she scarcely noticed the point at which it seemed to be somehow understood that she was going to be Dr. Heartbreak.

Books by Janice Harrell

Puppy Love
Heavens to Bitsy
Secrets in the Garden
Killebrew's Daughter
Sugar 'n' Spice
Blue Skies and Lollipops
Birds of a Feather
With Love from Rome
Castles in Spain
A Risky Business
Starring Susy
They're Rioting in Room 32
Love and Pizza to Go
B.J. on Her Own
Masquerade
Dear Dr. Heartbreak

JANICE HARRELL earned her M.A. and Ph.D. from the University of Florida, and for a number of years taught English at the college level. She is the author of a number of books for teens, as well as a mystery novel for adults. She lives in North Carolina.

JANICE HARRELL

Dear
Dr. Heartbreak

Keepsake
FROM
CROSSWINDS

CROSSWINDS

New York • Toronto • Sydney
Auckland • Manila

First publication October 1988

ISBN 0-373-88034-0

Dear Reader:

Welcome to our line of teen romances, Keepsake from Crosswinds. Here, as you can see, the focus is on the relationship between girls and boys, while the setting, story and the characters themselves contribute the variety and excitement you demand.

As always, your comments and suggestions are welcome.

The Editors
CROSSWINDS

Chapter One

"Sam, you're fantastic!" Luke said, his eyes glowing.

Samantha held up a hand like a traffic cop. "Don't say another word, Luke. Whatever it is you want me to do, I'm not about to."

"Okay," said Luke. He turned to idly flip a paper clip across the desk. "Forget I said anything." There was an awkward moment of silence, then he picked up his books to go.

Sam was surprised that he was giving up so quickly. She wished she hadn't cut him off before she had at least found out what he wanted her to do. It was the second time he had thrown a tantalizing hint her way, and she had to admit she was curious.

For a moment, Luke paused at the doorway of the classroom, leaning against the doorframe and smiling at her, his corn-silk pale hair a bright smudge against the darkness of the hall behind him. He wore old jeans, ripped and frayed at the knees, and even older sneakers from which his big toe peeked out, but the ragtag clothes did not make him any less attractive. That was part of the problem, Sam thought. As one of Luke's oldest friends, she was no sucker for his glittering good looks, but still when he started trying to get her to do something, she would inevitably feel herself starting to weaken, a difficulty she suspected she would not have had if he'd been ugly. The trouble was that the light in those blue eyes could be more persuasive than any reasonable argument. That was why it was sometimes better not even to look in his direction, much less listen to what he had to say.

"See ya," Luke said. He was out the door before Sam realized he had left without doing his share of the tagging and stacking of the school newspapers.

When she saw the tall stack that was left for her to do, she groaned. Resignedly she counted out thirty-two papers, wrapped twine around the bunch and stapled on a slip of paper with the name of a home-room teacher on it. Then she started on the next bundle.

She had almost finished sorting the entire stack into separate bundles for the homerooms when Pip showed up. "What's taking you so long?" he asked. "I thought you said you'd be finished about three-thirty."

"Luke took off before we finished, and I had to do it all myself."

"Typical," Pip replied. "Sam, haven't you ever noticed how you get the fuzzy end of the lollipop when that guy is around?"

"Not really. He just forgot. He didn't leave me with it on purpose."

"Ha!" Pip snorted. "I don't guess he's said anything more about that so-called secret proposition he had for you, has he? Because I've been thinking about it, and I don't think you ought to get involved in any of Luke's crazy ideas. You know I don't believe in telling people what they can and can't do, but I've got a very bad feeling about this. I want you to promise me whatever he wants you to do you won't do it."

Sam was conscious of a warm sense of virtue when she thought of how she had just cut Luke off as soon as he had started buttering her up. She had made a few mistakes in that direction in the past, helping Luke out when she shouldn't have, covering up for him when she should have let him crash, but that was behind her now. "Don't worry. I won't even listen to him."

"That's my girl," Pip said. He put his arm around her, drew her close and kissed her. But just when it was starting to get interesting, someone coughed.

"I hope I'm not interrupting anything," said Anita Jolley, not sounding sorry at all. She was standing at the door, her short, square bulk almost filling the doorway. "I think I left my chemistry book in here." She walked past Sam and Pip and bent down to look under a desk, the effort straining the seams of her skirt. When she straightened up, she was holding a chemistry book. "I passed Glamour Boy in the hall, but he didn't tell me you were in here."

Sam wasn't crazy about Anita's tone, but she was determined not to show it. "Do you know Pip?" Sam asked.

"Your boyfriend? We haven't been formally introduced, but I have seen you making out in the parking lot."

Sam decided to ignore the "making out" crack and the sneer that went with it. "Anita is one of the new staff members on the *Traveler*," Sam explained to Pip. "She was on the old *Cock and Bull*."

"I remember. The underground paper," Pip said. "So now you all are going to be on the regular newspaper staff?"

"Yeah, we were persuaded to 'come aboard'," Anita said. She pressed her chemistry book against her ample stomach. "Personally, I think it was a mistake for us to compromise our integrity by merging with the dippy school paper."

"Well, nobody's making you," said Sam, stung at last into a sharp retort.

"Except that Glamour Boy practically got down on his knees and begged us," said Anita. "I guess it bothered him that nobody was reading his boring old paper anymore." She lifted her foot and scraped a dusty loafer against her calf. "He told us we could be a paper within a paper if we came in with him and I'm holding him to it."

She pulled a newspaper out of a stack.

"Hey, I just got those all tied up," Sam protested. Anita gave no sign she had heard but spread the paper out on the desk next to Pip so that he could see that the page was peppered with small silhouettes of black roosters. "See, we're printing our logo next to every story written by one of the *Cock and Bull* staff," she explained. From where Sam stood the roosters gave the paper an alien look, as if the familiar *Traveler* had been invaded by giant bacteria.

"Not bad," Anita said, staring at the front page. "You see, now it's clear right away which stories the *Cock and Bull* people wrote. This way there's no chance people will get our stories mixed up with that rot the regular staffers write."

"Or vice versa," Pip said.

Anita looked surprised to be getting any back talk. She was probably accustomed to being around people who were more easily intimidated than Pip.

"You don't have to lock up the room, Anita," Sam said. "We leave it open for the janitorial staff." She took Pip's hand and fled.

"What's the hurry?" he protested as she pulled him down the hallway.

"I was afraid she was going to get mad at what you said."

"I hardly said anything. Besides, so what if she gets mad? What can she do to us?"

"Her being mad is bad enough."

"She can't kill us, Sam. Calm down."

"She goes out of her way to be nasty," Sam cried. "Why does she have to be that way?"

"Jealousy, I expect," Pip said. "Is she like that all the time?"

"Sure, she's like that all the time," Sam said glumly. "Third period is like civil war. Anita never lets us forget that she thinks they're all better than us. And Kilroy's just about as bad."

"Maybe it'll be better once you all get used to working together."

"Maybe."

Pip opened the door of his white Mercedes for her. It was a sunny day, and he had put the top of the car down.

"Sam, that stuff I said about Luke—I hope you don't think I said it because I'm jealous of him," he said, as he got in the other side. "Because it's not that way."

"Oh, I know that," she said, reaching for him.

He drew away. "You don't have to start reassuring me. I just told you I wasn't jealous."

"Good. Because it would be silly."

"Yeah, well, I was thinking about Mary Susan Swiderski, this girl I knew when we lived in Alexandria. I would always get my homework assignments from her, and what with one thing and another, she was over at the house a lot, but we were just friends. So what I'm saying is that I can grasp that that's all it is with you and Luke." He backed the car out of the parking place, adding under his breath, "Of course, Luke is a whole lot prettier than Mary Susan Swiderski."

"Dope," said Sam, grinning at him. They were driving down Thirteenth Street now, and the wind had begun blowing through her hair. Along the road the maples and oaks blazed orange and yellow against the blue of the sky and Sam could feel her spirits lifting. A true romantic, she often found that the real world fell short of her hopes. She would have liked to be a curvy brunette with masses of gypsy curls instead of a leggy blonde with hair that fell straight to her ears. She would have liked to have lived in Paris instead of smack in the middle of tobacco country in the dusty town of Fenterville. She would have liked for Pip to passionately kiss the arches of her feet instead of just saying, as he usually did, "Want to go by and pick up some fries?" In hundreds of ways Sam found that her world came up short, but this year at least the autumn leaves had not failed her. "Look at it!" she said, waving her arm. "Isn't it a gorgeous day? Ab-solutely gorgeous!"

Pip drove the convertible over a pile of leaves someone had raked onto the street. Leaves whirled behind them in the car's windy wake. "Nice," he agreed. "You know, when we moved here this summer, we drove in past all these rotting tobacco barns, chimneys standing in fields where farmhouses had burned down—Gothic decay was the flavor, if you get me. We had the air-conditioning on and the car was closed up tight as if we were passing through a contaminated zone. I was thinking I didn't like the looks of the place one bit and chills were already starting to creep up my spine. Then suddenly we came to this billboard—Repent for the Day of Judgment Is at Hand." He laughed. "What a welcome, right? I just about grabbed the steering wheel and turned the car around."

When Pip's grandfather had died, his father had given up his urban law practice and had brought his family to Fenterville to take over the family tobacco company. Sam knew the move had been a shock to Pip. In Fenterville the Byron Tobacco heir was like minor royalty. His privacy disappeared overnight. Perfect strangers in grocery stores and at filling stations gossiped about the car Pip drove and the girl he went out with. Pip was a private person by nature, and Sam suspected he had closed up a bit more since he had come to Fenterville. She was the only person at school he had gotten at all close to.

"Now I'm used to it," he went on. "Old tobacco barns don't faze me. I can even take ticky tacky subdivisions and the bums that hang out around the railroad tracks uptown. But I think they ought to take down that blinking sign and trade it in for one that doesn't give you goose bumps. How about something simple like Welcome to Fenterville? What's wrong with that? In my opinion this town would be better off with a little less local color.''

"You don't look to me like you're suffering much."

"It didn't take me long to notice some of the pretty parts around here," he said, looking at Sam.

It was warm, and Pip had pushed the sleeves of his shirt up, showing skin still dark with summer's tan. He had something of the coloring of his Spanish mother, with brown eyes and dark hair. Sam let her finger skate lightly along his forearm.

"I wish it could stay perfect like this!" she said.

"Nothing's ever perfect, Sam."

"Oh, I know that," she said shortly.

His words had reminded her with a jolt of the problems on the newspaper staff. It was true that nothing was perfect, but she was not going to let it spoil her day. It was bad enough that Anita was ruining third period without letting her ruin everything else, too. It was ridiculous to go crazy worrying about the newspaper. The staff couldn't go on fighting forever. Probably, things would work out somehow.

But that night, when Marcy called, it was pretty clear she did not share Sam's determined optimism.

"I don't know how much more I can take of Anita," Marcy said. "She came up to me this afternoon at the library, breathed a blast of garlic right in my face and started telling me what a rinky-dink outfit the *Traveler* was before the *Cock and Bull* staff joined up. I don't have to listen to that."

"I know," said Sam. "She came in when I was trying to get the papers packaged up and started in on me, too."

"But that's not all," Marcy said. "Listen to this. She actually went all sweetsie on me, and speaking to me in the kind voice you would use with some very slow child, she offered to help me out with my writing!"

In spite of herself, Sam found herself admiring Anita's nerve. "She was just trying to get to you."

"She got to me all right. I felt like crowning her with *Statistical Abstracts*. I wish I had. That would at least have put her out of commission for a while."

"Newspaper has gotten so grim," said Sam. "I mean, sometimes I look at Anita and Kilroy and I keep thinking they're going to rip off their disguises and yell 'trick or treat.' Do you think Anita ever washes her hair, Marcy? Ever?"

"My interest in Anita's personal hygiene is minimal."

"Well, I expect they have families that love them," Sam said doubtfully, "and they must have their own dreary little interests, investigating the sinkholes of society and writing zippy little articles or whatever, but you wouldn't exactly call them a laugh a minute, would you?"

"I would not. And if you ask me, Happy's adding her own nasty twist to the whole setup with the way she tries to snub them. Maybe the rest of us can giggle at that lady-of-the-manor act of hers, but I don't see those *Cock and Bull* kids laughing. Believe me, the way Happy is acting is not helping."

"Happy never helps," Sam said. "That's the one thing about the newspaper staff that never changes."

"What I'm trying to work up to saying, Sam, is that I'm going to drop off the newspaper."

"You can't do that!" cried Sam.

"I just don't need the grief. With my course load and working every day after school and trying to keep up with the clarinet, I'm overbooked. Newspaper was supposed to be a breathing space. Now it's like war!"

Sam's heart sank at the thought of being left friendless among the hostile factions of the newspaper staff. Luke would still be there, of course, but to give him credit, he was trying hard to steer a middle course between the opposing sides, as befitted his position as editor.

"But don't you remember how we promised Luke we wouldn't let him down?" Sam cried. "How we said we were behind him all the way now that he was editor?"

"He's got plenty of staff. In fact, now that we've taken in the *Cock and Bull* people, we've really got too many people. There's not that much for any of us to do."

"So newspaper's not adding to your work load, then, is it?" said Sam triumphantly. "You could stay on."

"It's the staff meetings that are getting me down, not the work. I've already talked to Luke about it."

Sam caught her breath. So Marcy was really serious about this, then. It wasn't just that she was feeling a little low.

"Luke said he understood," said Marcy. "And that I should do what I had to do. He said he knew I had a lot weighing on me, and he didn't want me to make myself crazy."

"At least think it over some," Sam begged.

"Oh, I will. But I just don't know how much more I can take."

"Hang in there, Marce. It's got to get better."

But after she hung up, Sam was forced to admit she couldn't think of a single reason why it should.

"Sam!" her mother called up the stairs. "Luke's here."

Sam hurried downstairs. "He didn't want to come in?"

"He said he'd wait for you out front."

Sam ran out the front door and found Luke sitting on the porch swing in half darkness. She could hear the faint creak of the swing as it moved. His face looked yellow in the light of the bug-proof porch lamp and crazy shadows were moving on the porch as the swing went back and forth.

"I've just been talking to Marcy," Sam said. "She's telling me she wants to quit the newspaper staff."

"I talked to her myself," Luke replied. "Pretty bad isn't it? Okay, Sam, what do you say? Are you ready to listen to my proposition?"

Chapter Two

Don't worry," Luke said with heavy sarcasm. "It's not anything Pip wouldn't want you to do."

Sam frowned at him. "You don't have to act like I'm Pip's slave. I've got a mind of my own."

"I haven't noticed much sign of it since Pip came to town."

"Cut it out, Luke! I don't go giving you advice on your girlfriends, do I? Not even when Jenny Halstead was two-timing you all over town."

Luke winced.

"So let's just leave Pip out of this, okay?" Sam said.

"Out of it is just where I want him to be, Sam. The thing is, for this to work, it's got to be a complete secret. Nobody, and I mean nobody, can know about it. Not Pip. Not even Marcy."

"This isn't something illegal, is it?" asked Sam.

"No, nothing like that. But you know how it is. As soon as you tell one person it's all over school. This is going to be just between you and me, the two of us."

Sam knew that Pip wouldn't like her sharing a secret with Luke. Also she had resolved not to get involved in any of Luke's schemes, but the situation was suddenly looking more desperate than it had earlier. Marcy was talking about bailing out. If Luke thought he had a solution to the way the newspaper staff had deteriorated, Sam was ready to listen to him. After all, she told herself, if what he proposed sounded like a bad idea, she could always say no.

She took a deep breath. "Okay, go on."

"The problem we've got with the newspaper staff," Luke said, "is that we've lost all balance."

"The problem is that the *Cock and Bull* staff are a bunch of creeps, that's what."

"Not a helpful attitude, Sam. We've got to analyze this thing and find a solution."

Luke produced a copy of the *Traveler* from the shadows and shook it open. Sam could barely make out the print in the dim yellow light of the front porch, but Luke seemed to have no problem reading it. Such was his obsession with the paper that it crossed Sam's mind that he might have the whole front page memorized.

"Okay, here's this week's *Traveler*," he said. "Visit to a Tattoo Parlor by Kilroy. Teenaged Felons: Is Rehabilitation a Farce? by Anita. Inside Black Sabbath by Richard Evans. All snappy stories by the *Cock and Bull* staff. Now look at the stuff the regular staff is putting out. We did a profile of the new math teacher. It's not our fault Mr. Gravelly is dull, but there it is, a dull story. Next, an explanation of the overrun in cost and the delay in the construction schedule of the new band room, also dull. Then, a rundown on the football team's hopes for the upcoming season, not exactly breathtaking. Finally my story on what goes into the cafeteria meat loaf, which would have been more exciting if some of the things we suspected were in the meat loaf had actually been in it. Okay, do you see the problem? Those *Cock and Bull* staffers don't have any respect for us because the traditional type stories that we're doing seem boring to them. They figure we just can't cut it.''

"But a lot more people care about the football team than about the local tattoo parlor, Luke. Nobody I know goes to a tattoo parlor, except Kilroy. The regular staff is covering stuff that the kids want to hear about.''

"You know that and I know that, Sam, but those *Cock and Bull* people have got the idea that they're holding the paper afloat all by themselves.''

"They're conceited, all right.''

"What we need is a traditional column with drop-dead appeal. Nothing sophisticated or intellectual, just a mainline type column, but one that will knock everybody's socks off. I want something that even the *Cock and Bull* kids will have to admit is drawing in more readers than their stuff.''

"You've got something in mind?''

"Yup. I do. But what I want you to remember is that it's not so much what we do, but how we promote it that counts. What sold the pet rock? What made Vanna White a star? What rocketed roach hotels to success?''

"You've got me.''

"Hype, Sam, hype. This thing is going to need a big buildup."

"Where do I fit in?" asked Sam. She was watching him closely, waiting for the inevitable catch to appear.

"You're going to write it. It's going to be an advice column."

"I don't see what's so secret about that. Lots of papers have advice columns." A sudden qualm struck her. "But I'm not sure I could write one, now that I think of it. It sounds tricky."

"You'd be perfect for it. You're patient, you're sympathetic, you understand people."

Sam had the uncomfortable feeling she was being buttered up again, but when she analyzed what Luke had said word by word she had to admit that it was true.

"More important," he added, "you don't have a distinctive writing style. You see, nobody is going to know that you're writing it. If they know it's only you they won't have any respect for the column."

"Thanks a lot!"

"I didn't mean that! All I mean is that nobody takes anything seriously when they know that whoever doing it is just another junior at Lee High. Complete anonymity is basic. I've got it all figured out."

Later on, looking back, Sam could not remember exactly agreeing to the plan. In fact, she scarcely noticed the point at which it seemed to be somehow understood that she was going to be Dr. Heartbreak.

"I hope I can write something like that," she said uneasily.

"You'll be terrific. You see, we'll *create* this Dr. Heartbreak. This guy will have his own personality, his own voice. We'll have people send their letters to a box number and you can mail your column in to the school. That way you preserve the secrecy. Piece of cake. Dr. Heartbreak will capture the interest of the entire school, I promise you.''

''But you actually think this is going to solve our problems with Anita and those kids? I don't quite see it. I mean, why should this make any difference?''

''They need humility, right? This column is going to teach them humility.''

''I guess they could use some of that, all right.''

Sam was a little chagrined when the very next day signs appeared all over school advertising the upcoming column by Dr. Heartbreak. The signs were not just the usual tempera and poster-board affairs, either. It looked as if they had been done by a silk-screen process. They were sophisticated looking, almost luminous. It was a little unsettling for her to realize that while she was still promising herself she wouldn't even listen to Luke, he was already having the posters made up.

She stared at the one that was taped to the wall near her locker. It said:

Coming Soon! Dr. Heartbreak's column of advice in the *Traveler*. Tell your problems to Dr. Heartbreak, P.O. Box 3228, Fenterville. All communications kept confidential.

The sign was decorated with a lurid blue heart that seemed to shine and pulse with life, as if it might any moment drip blue blood. On top of the heart, incongruously, lay a pair of horn-rim glasses.

Sam was struck with a sudden wave of something very like panic as she stood facing the poster. Dr. Heartbreak. That was her!

She felt even worse later when she saw the one outside her English class. Again, there was that strange looking blue heart with the horn-rim glasses and under it the caption:

Dr. Heartbreak listens. Parents don't understand you? Friends don't appreciate you? Are you hassled from morning to night? Get professional advice from Dr. Heartbreak.

Professional advice? Taken together with the "Dr. Heartbreak" label, Sam realized that might make people think she was a trained counselor. Was this the catch Pip had warned her would appear sooner or later in anything Luke thought up?

"Luke!" she yelped, as she saw him pass her. "We've got to talk!"

He looked around as if searching for some way to escape her, but Sam backed him into a corner by his locker.

"*Professional*," she said, "means like my mom the social worker, or a doctor or a psychologist or a chiropractor or somebody like that. You can't say I give professional advice!"

"Keep your voice down," he implored her. "It's just an expression, like when they advertise Dr. Bill the transmission specialist. Nobody thinks Dr. Bill went to medical school. Don't take it so seriously."

"That sign has got to come down," she insisted. "It's false advertising."

"All advertising is false advertising. Those signs cost money, you know, and I'm paying for them out of my own pocket."

But Sam would not give way. At last, they reached a compromise. Luke did not take down the offending sign, but he did clarify it. He hastily cut the heart design off another poster and taped it to fresh poster board with a new message. Sam saw it a bit later, posted by the cafeteria door.

Suffering from generation gap? Need a cool, clear outlook on your problems from someone *your own age*, someone who really understands your situation—write Dr. Heartbreak!

The blue heart above the message seemed to pulse ominously. Just looking at it had come to make Sam vaguely uneasy.

"Would someone be so kind as to tell me what's going on with this Dr. Heartbreak thing?" Happy asked at the staff meeting. "I realize I am *only* the assistant editor, but I do think I'm entitled not to be the very last to know what is going on around here. I mean, do you mind?"

"The *Traveler* is about to sink to ever new depths," said Anita. "That's all. Anytime you need something explained, Happy hon, just ask me."

Happy lifted her porcelain-white nose a shade higher. She had gotten in the habit lately of sitting on the table so as to be able to look down at the staff members who were sitting in chairs and desks.

Kilroy fingered the Mohawk brush that ran like a stiff cockscomb down the middle of his bare scalp. A used plastic lighter dangled from one of his ears and when he crossed his legs, one could not help noticing his trademark red elevator shoes. "Who's the lucky bimbo who gets to put out this junk?" he asked. "Tracy and Danita going to do it in their spare time, huh?"

"What's that supposed to mean?" said Danita, facing him boldly. "Just because Tracy and I are the typists doesn't mean we're dumb, you know. I'm getting pretty sick of being treated like a second-class citizen around here, aren't you, Tracy?"

Luke put his arm around Danita. "Hey, Kilroy's just spouting off, Dan. He doesn't mean it. How many words a minute do you type, Kilroy? Because we can't get along without Danita and Tracy, you know. They're the ones that hold things together around here."

Kilroy mumbled something that could have been either an apology or a curse.

Mr. Perkins, their faculty adviser, who might have been able to bring a little calm to the proceedings, was out at another of his many dental appointments. Since the *Cock and Bull* staff had come aboard, his teeth had deteriorated amazingly. Sam privately suspected him of holing up in the downtown library where he could mark his class papers in peace.

"I don't know why I can't be the one to do the new column," Felicia complained.

"I suppose Luke is giving it to one of his special friends," said Happy, looking pointedly at Sam and Marcy.

"I don't know who's doing it," Luke said.

This remark got everyone's attention. The staff looked at Luke blankly for a moment, and Sam did her best to look surprised, too.

Felicia began speaking very quickly. "If you haven't made up your mind yet who's going to do it, I want to say that I have a special expertise in the advice-column area because I am taking a psychology course. Also, it should go to an underclassperson because it will probably take up a lot of time, and you may want it to go on for years. If a sophomore wrote it, it would have more continuity."

"Hey, wait a minute, here—" protested Reggie.

"It's not going to be staff written," Luke said. "It's more like a syndicated column. I just got this offer in the mail. I figured, what do we have to lose? We'll take a flyer on it."

"So," Happy said, examining a perfect pink nail. "Rushing in without a *moment's* thought, as usual. You don't know anything about this person, what his credentials are, what his writing is like, whether he's emotionally stable, or whether he sets a good example, just to name a *few* items that might be of concern."

"I'm not marrying the guy, Happy," Luke said. "I'm just publishing his column. Don't forget, I'll still be editing it. If anything's not strictly on the up and up, I can always cut it out."

Sam did not like the way Marcy was looking at Luke. It was pretty clear that she didn't believe his story about the syndicated columnist. That was hardly surprising. It sounded pretty thin to Sam, too. But at least Marcy was too loyal to undercut Luke in front of all the others.

"You really don't know who does this column?" Reggie asked. "Honest, Luke? Have you checked this thing out with Mr. Perkins?"

"I appreciate all the concern, guys," Luke said. "But I have checked it out with Mr. Perkins. He said he'd probably want to look the columns over, too. I expect to have the first one in the next edition. Then you can make up your own minds about it."

The oddly assorted staff looked at him with settled expressions of discontent. For the moment, however, nobody was insulting anybody, nobody's voice was raised. Luke had got their attention, if nothing else.

Even Pip, who missed a lot of what was going on at Lee because he was still rather new, had not missed seeing the signs about the upcoming column. Sam learned that when they sat down under the Wishing Tree with their lunch. "What's this Dr. Heartbreak stuff that's plastered all over school?" Pip asked, stretching his long legs out on the grass.

"A new advice column," Sam said. "Luke's keeping it a big secret who's writing it. He says it's some sort of syndicated column, but Marcy told me she thinks he's writing it himself."

"Luke writing an advice column? Hasn't he skated on the edge of being kicked out of school most of his natural life? This is our advice columnist?"

"His sense of humor may have gotten a little out of hand a few times, Pip, but I keep trying to tell you he's reformed since he's gotten to be editor of the *Traveler*. He really cares about the newspaper."

"I hear you," Pip said doubtfully.

"I think Marcy's wrong, though. I don't think he's writing it," Sam said.

"He's sure giving it enough publicity," Pip said, biting into his sandwich. "Seeing that blue heart right outside the cafeteria just about puts you off your food."

The school buzzed with speculation about the proposed new column the rest of that day and the next. But when, at the end of the week, Sam and Luke went to Dr. Heartbreak's post office box, they found it completely empty. Sam looked at Luke in dismay. "Nobody's sending us their problems! What are we going to do? We'll have to cancel the column."

"Not on your life. We'll make up some letters, that's all. Just go home and write up both the questions and answers. Piece of cake."

Later Sam thought about Luke's solution with some resentment as she sat down at her father's typewriter. "Make up some letters." It was easy to say. Wasn't it bad enough that she had to give the advice without her having to come up with the problems on top of it? Looking at the sheet of paper in the typewriter seemed to paralyze her mind. It was so incredibly blank.

She fished her trusty spiral-bound notebook out of her purse. At least that paper had some lines on it, so it didn't look so dauntingly empty. She pulled out her red felt-tip pen and began making a list. Order and method—that was the secret to getting anything done. She wrote:

1. Love
2. Power
3. Fame
4. Wealth

Then she sucked on her felt-tip pen and surveyed her list with satisfaction. Lists were truly amazing. Moments ago she had had zip, but now with the help of her list she had summed up all the major human passions. She only had to translate them into high school terms.

After some thought she changed her list so that it read

1. Love
2. Grades
3. Popularity
4. Clothes, cars

Now she was getting somewhere. She would begin with a letter on love, which was, when it came to passions, her personal favorite. She began to type.

Dear Dr. Heartbreak,
I want my boyfriend to say he is crazy about me but all he ever says is something like, "Want some french fries?" He is not the demonstrative type. What can I do?

Hopeful

Dear Hopeful,
Dear child in distress, be patient. Love is a tender plant that must be allowed to slowly unfold in its own season. Try to understand your beloved's fear of ridicule, his holding back from saying things he fears might go the rounds at school. *Go on loving him.* Remember that some natures are as delicate as spring flowers. They are none the less sincere for that.

Not bad, she thought, reading over it. She had written an answer to her own problem, which had to show she was getting on top of this thing. She was getting a feel for Dr. Heartbreak, too. A big wet sponge of sympathy—that was the way she saw him.

Sam proceeded to the next item on her list, "popularity," and began typing rapidly.

Dear Dr. Heartbreak,
A while ago I got myself a rat-and-snake tattoo. It's done in three colors, and it's a real work of art. Like, when I flex my biceps you can see those suckers move. Since I got my tattoo nobody wants to sit next to me in biology. This bozo in my gym class tells me I should get a skin graft, but I'm not about to give up my tattoo just to suit some finky snobs in this rotten school. What do you think?

Killer

Dear Killer,
We all hunger and thirst for friendship. Reading between the lines of your letter, I can see that you, too, long for friendship. Do not think the less of yourself for that. It is *all right* for you to want finky snobs to like you. You ask if a skin graft is necessary. To find the answer ask yourself these questions—Have I been holding the dissecting knife in an unnecessarily threatening manner? Do I suffer from halitosis?

If the answer to both of these questions is a resounding no, then perhaps your tattoo is indeed the problem. May I suggest long-sleeved shirts?

"Sam?"
Hearing her mother's voice, Sam hastily ripped the

page out of the typewriter and hid it under her note-book before the door to the study opened.

"Dinner, sweetheart."

Sam's father taught history at Lee High, which, as Sam saw it, had the potential for blighting her entire high school career. She and her father had made a pact that he would try not to interfere unduly in her life at school and generally, their agreement worked pretty well. Still, there were times he asked questions Sam would just have soon he hadn't, and tonight was obviously going to be one of those times.

"What's this Dr. Heartbreak they're advertising all over the place?" her father asked after they sat down at the table.

"A new column in the newspaper," Sam said. She showered her spaghetti with Parmesan.

"You should see the signs, Ginny," her father told her mother. "Surrealistic. Very cleverly done. The kind of thing that curls your hair. Is this column going to review horror films or what, Sam?"

"Advice column," Sam mumbled, her mouth full.

"An advice column?" said Sam's mother. "I don't like the sound of that. When people have problems they should seek professional help, not go writing some fellow student who is just as confused as they are. Who's doing this column?"

"It's a secret. Don't worry, Mom, it's not anything serious. They'll probably just make up the letters, anyway. Who'd be dumb enough to write to an advice column?" She thought ruefully of the empty post office box. "It's just for fun."

"Don't take it so seriously, Ginny," said Sam's father. "My feeling is that anything would be better than reading about the deplorable sanitary conditions in the local tattoo parlors.''

Sam's fork paused midway to her mouth. Tattoo parlor. It had suddenly hit her that it was Kilroy's article about tattoo parlors that had given her the idea for the last letter she had written. She was going to have to watch that kind of thing or she could be given away by the telltale train of associations in her mind. Maybe, she thought, she should use random words in the dictionary as a takeoff place for the letters. The only trouble was it was hard enough to think up letters at all without having to think up one based on weird words like ''photosynthesis.''

Twin parallel lines had appeared between her mother's eyebrows. ''I just hope if this Dr. Heartbreak gets any real problems he'll have the good sense to refer them to a professional.''

''Oh, I'm sure he will, Mom.'' Sam added hastily, ''I mean, not that I know anything about it, but I'm sure he would, if anything like that should come up. I mean, it's absolutely completely harmless.''

''I hope you're right,'' said her mother, frowning.

Chapter Three

When the next edition of the *Traveler* came out, everyone in the school seemed to turn first to Dr. Heartbreak's column. Putting up all those signs had paid off.

"You're on the newspaper staff, aren't you, Sam? Who writes this Heartbreak column?" Bill Finch asked Sam as they were leaving homeroom.

"It's a sort of syndicated column," Sam said. "We get it from outside. What did you think of it?"

"Soppy," was Bill's judgment.

At this Sam drooped a little, but during algebra she saw some people reading the column. That had to be a good sign.

When she got to the staff room third period, Anita was slumped in her desk, looking deflated. "Now I believe it," Anita croaked. "Your average newspaper reader has the I.Q. of an 8-year-old. All day nobody was reading anything except that stupid column. What about my analysis of the parole system? I might as well have put it in a bottle and thrown it off a pier.''

"I could have written a better advice column," said Felicia, fidgeting with her glasses. She had exchanged her usual contact lenses for the glasses in an apparent last-ditch effort to convince Luke she was wise enough to write an advice column. "My psychology course is giving me a whole lot of insight into the bizarre workings of the human mind. For example, I would say that boy named Killer should get in touch with his unconscious hostility. It's perfectly clear that's why he had the tattoo done in the first place—all that unconscious hostility. It's no coincidence that this boy has no friends."

Sam was spellbound by this insightful analysis of Killer's motives. For a second she almost forgot that Killer was a product of her own imagination.

"Honestly, Luke," Happy said, "I hope you didn't pay for that column in advance. Because if you did I would almost call it a misuse of the Student Activity Fee." She frowned at a chip she had discovered on the polish of her thumbnail. "It's a case of the blind leading the blind, as far as I can see. Why would any sane person write a perfect stranger to get advice? It's stupid."

"Oh, I don't know," said Sam. "It can help to get a fresh viewpoint sometimes."

Happy lifted the newspaper. "I suppose you wrote this one, Marcy. 'Dear Dr. Heartbreak, Just because I have the top grade point average in my class, people act as if I'm some sort of freak. I have to make good grades if I am ever going to get the scholarship I need to go to a good college. Should I have to apologize for that? What can I do to make people realize I'm a human being, too?' It's signed, 'Toots.'"

Everyone turned to look at Marcy, and she flushed under their gaze. "No, I didn't write it," she said. "And if you can picture me calling myself 'Toots' then you've got one terrific imagination, that's all I can say."

"I thought that part about how she has trouble persuading people that she's a human being rang a bell," said Happy.

"Very funny, Happy," said Marcy. "No, it wasn't me. The only thing is—"

"We see what you're trying to say," Kilroy put in. "Around here nobody else's grades are as good as yours, memsahib. But has it hit you that some of the humble peons on the lower levels have their own problems, huh?"

Marcy was looking puzzled. "I guess it could have been a sophomore. Or it could have been Tony Margulis. He's a senior and all set to be valedictorian this year, but I don't see how it could be Tony because his father's an oral surgeon and he doesn't need a scholarship. Of course, if it's a syndicated column, the letter could come from some other school." She frowned. "Yes, that's got to be it. It's a letter from another school."

Sam was holding her breath. It had seemed only natural to use Marcy's problems in the column since she was so familiar with them. But now she could see how risky it had been. Luckily, it had all worked out for the best since that letter seemed to have convinced Marcy that the column was coming from outside, but she was going to have to watch it in the future.

"The whole thing is junk," said Anita. "It's got about the same intellectual content as mud wrestling."

"You may have a point there, Anita," said Felicia, peering earnestly through her glasses. "This sort of column appeals to the voyeur element in people's psychology."

"I liked it," Tracy said in a small voice.

At these few kind words, it was all Sam could do to keep from falling on Tracy's neck with tears of gratitude.

Sam and Marcy walked together to gym after third period. "I was all wrong about Luke writing that advice column," Marcy told Sam. "As soon as I read it I knew that. Can you picture Luke writing, 'my dearest child'? Oh, it's one of those syndicated things, all right. I feel awful about not believing him. I hope this isn't a sinister sign that I'm working too hard, Sam. You know, the first crack in the facade that presages paranoia, suspicion, total disintegration of the personality."

"You're always working too hard," said Sam, trotting to keep up with her. "Why would your personality pick now to disintegrate?"

"Maybe it's the atmosphere of third period that's doing it to me." Marcy restlessly pushed her dark hair behind her ears with her free hand. "Maybe I'm getting so I can't tell my friends apart from Happy and Anita and all the others. After all, the one thing I know is that I can trust you and Luke and if I start thinking you're hiding things from me, then I must be going around the bend."

Guilt struck Sam's heart like a stake. While it was true, she told herself, that she wasn't exactly lying—

just holding back a few facts—she wasn't sure that Marcy would see it that way if the truth came out. Not that it was going to come out, she reminded herself. Nobody seemed exactly crazy about the column, so they would probably do just one or two more columns and then quietly fade it out.

"The only thing I can't figure out," Marcy said as she pushed open the door of the locker room, "is that if it is syndicated, the way Luke said, then why is the address a local box number?"

"Maybe Luke collects the stuff up and sends it on."

"I guess that must be it," Marcy said. But she looked abstracted as she groped in her gym bag for her socks. "I'll have to ask him how he does it."

After this little chat, Sam could not wait to end the Dr. Heartbreak column. But when she saw Luke just before chemistry, she discovered that he was looking at it quite differently.

"What do you mean nobody liked it, Sam? They kept talking about it the whole period, didn't they? It made an impact. Sure they knocked it. But that's just jealousy. Let me tell you, the kids were eating it up, couldn't get enough of it. Everywhere I looked all day people were reading it. Just keep in mind that everybody always puts down hits. When's the last time you heard somebody say something nice about roach hotels?"

The day so far had not been exactly an ego builder and it did not help to have Luke comparing her column to a roach hotel.

"Anita and Happy were just as nasty as ever," Sam pointed out. "I don't see that we're getting anywhere."

"You can't expect miracles. Anita looked kind of down today, didn't she? And she wasn't tooting her own horn so much, either. I'll bet she's starting to see that there's a lot more to selling papers than she figured."

Luke looked as sleek as a cat licking the last few crumbs of salmon off his mouth. Sam realized that it was in Luke's nature to enjoy deceiving people. It appealed to his sense of humor. No doubt it was this taste for intrigue that blinded him to the fact that the column had been a flop. "Just watch it when you make up those problems, Sam," he cautioned. "I spotted your problem and Marcy's problem myself. If one of mine shows up the next time people might start to put two and two together."

Sam blushed. She wondered how Luke had guessed that the first letter had been her problem.

"I'll watch it," she assured him. Later she realized she should have said, "Forget it!" She should have said, "If you're so particular about how it's done, write it yourself."

Sam went by the post office box again on Friday night. She didn't really have much hope that anybody had written to Dr. Heartbreak, but she was in a tight corner. Thinking up problems that revealed nothing about herself was very tough. In view of that, she figured it was worth checking the box just in case.

When she spun the combination lock and opened the little metal and glass door, to her surprise she saw that the box was stuffed tight with envelopes. Tugging, she managed at last to dislodge a few and then the rest came tumbling out with them. Some of them slipped to the floor and a little slip of paper fluttered a way off. Sam scooped up the letters and retrieved the bit of paper. It read "Postal Patron—Patrons who receive a large volume of mail are advised to rent a postal drawer. See your postal clerk for further information. Postmaster."

A large volume of mail, Sam thought wonderingly. Luke had been right. The column was a success after all.

Sam's buoyant spirits lasted at least until she got home, and she realized she was going to have to read all that mail. She called Luke up at home and told him to come over.

He arrived almost at once, bursting into her father's study so suddenly that the draft from the door sent some of the envelopes flying to the floor.

"The post office wants us to get a larger box," Sam said.

"Holy Toledo," he said, staring at the pile of letters. "Do you see what this means, Sam?"

"A lot of work," Sam said.

"Think of all those readers pouring out their hearts to you on paper. You can't let them down. You've got to answer these letters! That way we get a lot of good will toward the paper. Geez, it's better than advertising for stirring up interest in the paper and you saw what we did with advertising."

"There's no way I could answer all these," said Sam. "It would take hours. When would I ever get my homework done or see Pip? Besides, a lot of them don't even have return addresses. We're not the only ones who like anonymity."

Luke ran his fingers over the stack of letters like a gambler lovingly checking the deck for marked cards. "I've got it," he said. "What we'll do is in the next paper we'll announce an added service. People who want a private response can send three bucks and a stamped, self-addressed envelope.''

"Three dollars? Why would anybody pay three dollars for my advice?"

"Look at it this way. We're going to have to get a P.O. drawer. Our expenses are going up. And I still owe Barnabas Printing for half the cost of those signs. Think about it. We're not twisting anybody's arm. We're just offering an extra service, purely optional, for the people who want it."

Sam looked at the big stack of mail. It did seem a little coldhearted just to leave her fans hanging when they were counting on her answer.

"You'll help me?" she asked.

"For sure. You can count on me."

"Well, all right."

Luke smiled radiantly. "We'll tell them Dr. Heartbreak's added special service in the next paper. I have to say, Sam, this thing is succeeding beyond my wildest dreams. We're onto something here. Je-rusalem. It's great."

When Luke left, Sam began working her way through the letters. The first six were from girls wanting to know how to get guys to notice them. Sam tossed them into a single pile. Unrequited Lust, she privately dubbed them. She was beginning to see the fun side to being Dr. Heartbreak. She got a kick out of knowing other people's secrets. She supposed Felicia would call that the voyeuristic element in her psychology. But the best part was submerging her own identity into the all-understanding mind of Dr. Heartbreak. When Sam was writing Dr. Heartbreak's answers she felt calmer and wiser than Sam Morrison. Dr. Heartbreak didn't sit around feeling insecure. He wasn't eaten up with guilt just for carrying on a small deception of his friends. He was on top of it all. Cool. Sam saw him as tall and robust, with masses of black gypsy curls. He had probably lived abroad a good deal, in Paris. That was how he achieved his Olympian detachment.

Sam got a small electric shock when she picked up the next letter. She knew that handwriting—delicate, very sloping and in light blue ink. It was so familiar. In a minute she was sure she would be able to place it.

She tore open the envelope, catching a whiff of perfume in the process.

Dear Dr. Heartbreak,
I am an intelligent, beautiful sixteen-year-old and *exceptionally* mature for my age. My boyfriend is the star quarterback of the football team, a tall, deeply tanned senior who is almost too handsome to live, to be perfectly blunt about it.

Sam sucked in her breath. Happy had written it! Who else was dating Jim Shipman, the star quarterback? Happy always shopped the football team for her boyfriends because she liked them burly and famous, and Jim was widely thought to be her greatest catch. Sam read on.

Anyone looking at me would imagine I have absolutely everything a girl could want or need. Sophomores have even told me how lucky I am to be in the "in crowd." That is the cruel irony, Dr. Heartbreak. I am *not* really in that crowd. Oh, it may look that way to the sophomores because I know all the kids in the in group and I certainly should be in that crowd, but I am always on the outside looking in. I get asked to the big parties, but not to the intimate little get-togethers that really count.

I deserve better, but that's the story of my life. My parents have always liked my big sister best and they let my baby sister get away with murder. Nobody in my family even notices me unless I make them. Everything I've ever had in this life I've had to fight for and it's not fair! What can I do to make people appreciate me?

Beauty

Sam found it fascinating to get this glimpse into her enemy's mind. Who would have dreamed that Happy looked on herself as a victim? It made Sam a little curious about the diary of Ivan the Terrible. He probably thought everybody was picking on him, too.

She laid the letter down. What a surprise to find Happy writing! Listening to her tearing down the column, who would have guessed she was gearing herself up to seek Dr. Heartbreak's advice?

Of course, that she had written showed that she had bought hook, line and sinker Luke's story about the column being syndicated, and Sam felt a little ashamed about the deception when she looked at it that way. But the feeling faded quickly when she remembered some of the dirty tricks Happy had pulled in the past.

It is hard to answer sympathetically a letter your worst enemy has written complaining about you, but Sam felt she had to try. She rolled a sheet of paper into the typewriter.

Dear Beauty,

My dear child, the old advice is still the best advice—the way to have a friend is to be one. You say you want to be a part of this crowd but you do not say whether you really like any of these people. If you do not, they may sense your dislike. They may even sense that you are angry at them for failing to recognize your many good qualities. Anger is, alas, no basis for friendship. If I may offer you advice, and believe my child, only with your best interests at heart, it would be to avoid thinking of your social life as a status contest. Look for shared interests, similar points of view and genuine affection when you seek friendship and you will reap, I promise you, golden rewards.

Sam gave a satisfied sigh as she rummaged through the stack of letters. She was pleased at the way her professionalism had risen above her dislike of Happy. None of the other envelopes bore familiar handwriting, which was just as well. It had been interesting to get Happy's letter, but she could see it could get sticky if people you knew started writing for advice. You could get into a conflict of interest situation that way. There was a rap on the study door and Sam jumped. "Sam?" called her mother. "Pip's here."

Quickly Sam threw her sweater over the stack of letters. Her date with Pip had completely slipped her mind.

Pip peeked in the door. "Are you going to wear that to the movies?" he asked, eyeing her old jeans. "It's fine with me if that's what you want to do but—"

"I've got to go dress. My watch must have stopped. I'll run up and change."

"Let me look at that watch," said Pip. "Maybe you just pulled out the wind button or something."

Sam scooted by him very fast so he could not see her watch. "Not now. I'll be back in a minute," she called over her shoulder as she charged up the stairs.

She hoped her mother wasn't going to tidy up in the study and put the navy sweater away. She was pretty sure she was safe. After her parents had put in a hard week at work, the last thing they were likely to do on a Friday night was to go on a cleaning binge. In fact, Sam's father was fond of saying that their household habitually hovered one step above squalor.

Upstairs, Sam quickly changed into her best sweater and skirt, not forgetting to turn her watch back an hour and pull out the stem. Then she ran a brush quickly through her hair and ran downstairs.

Pip took her wrist and held it up to the light. "Hey!" he said triumphantly. "You did leave the stem out. That's why it stopped." He pressed the stem back in with his thumb, then held her jacket for her while she slipped into it. "Want to do anything special after the movies?" he asked.

Yes, she thought. You may strew my path with rose petals, waltz with me by moonlight and sing to me while a thousand violins play our love song.

"We could go by Hardee's afterward and get some fries," he suggested.

They drove off in elegant quiet in the white car. The night had turned chill and Pip had the heater on. The Mercedes was rather like Pip, Sam thought—smooth, strong, and giving off an aura of money that was hard to pin down.

Pip, his arm around her, steered with one hand. Sam shivered a little and snuggled up close to him so that her nose was up against his hair. She caught the scent of whatever it was he put on it, and underneath the faint warm smell that was his alone, which she loved.

"Did you read that new column in the paper?" he asked. "The Heartbreak thing?"

She was afraid he could feel her stiffening. "I skimmed it," she said.

"What did you think of it?"

Sam cleared her throat. "Well, that sort of thing does appeal to people's voyeuristic instincts, don't you think? And then there's a kind of superficiality and glibness to the whole thing."

"I liked it."

She realized her mouth had fallen open, and she hastily closed it. "You did?"

"What's so funny about that? I like reading about other people's problems. Either the problem looks like something only an idiot could have gotten himself into—I mean a rat-and-snake tattoo, you've got to be kidding, right? Or else it's something pretty easy to fix."

"It's not so easy when they're your own problems," said Sam, thinking of her own advice to herself—"let the tender plant of love unfold at its own season." All very well to say that, but if she was waiting for Pip to act like Lord Cavendish in *Love's Savage Adventure*, she suspected she would have to wait the rest of her life.

"Everything's simpler on paper," Pip said. "I've noticed that. In a column like that, you'll notice that any problem in the world can be wrapped up in six or seven lines. Instead of Dr. Heartbreak they should call the thing Easy Answers.''

Sam wondered what he would think if he found out that she was the one dishing out the easy answers.

Chapter Four

I sense a definite change in the mood of the student body," declared Happy, smoothing an eyebrow with her pinkie. "Back in the days of the *Cock and Bull*, the people were interested in offbeat stories. But now they want stories from the *heart*, stories that touch the full range of everyday experience. I am sure I could write that kind of story." Her eyes glazed over with thought.

Nor was she the only pensive one in the room. Marcy's chin was resting on her hand. The day was gloomy, and under the overhead light the dark bangs which covered her eyebrows seemed to cast her eyes in shadow. *"Sic transit gloria mundi,"* she said.

"English, pu-lease," said Happy. "I mean, do you *mind*?"

"I mean easy come, easy go," said Marcy. "Roughly."

Anita could not have enjoyed listening to Happy and Marcy treat the *Cock and Bull* as if it were an outmoded antique, but the runaway success of Dr. Heartbreak's column had put her in a low enough mood that she didn't even answer back. She sat slumped in her desk twirling a stringy bit of hair around her forefinger.

Happy looked down at the copy of the *Traveler* draped over her knees. "What is it that touches the human heart?" she asked, gesturing largely with one hand.

"Acid indigestion," said Anita sourly.

Happy ignored her. "If I were starting a paper now," she said, "I'd want to do something soft and rather sentimental, a kind of *pastel* paper. Take this first letter in the Heartbreak column, the one signed 'Beauty.' Here is a story with potential, a beautiful gifted girl besieged on all sides by her enemies, misunderstood even by Dr. Heartbreak, to whom she turned for advice. I see it as a series. Illustrated in color."

Kilroy groaned and held his hand to his head. "You've got to be kidding. That Beauty chick is so full of herself she wouldn't blow away in a high wind."

Happy smiled sweetly. "It is differences of opinion that make a horse race, I believe."

"Horse race?" said Kilroy. "Horse—"

"That will do, Kilroy," said Mr. Perkins from the corner where he was marking papers. That Mr. Perkins had returned from the dentist's chair was as good a sign as any, Sam thought, of the improved atmosphere in the newsroom. If perfect peace was not the rule, at least the hostilities were in a lower key.

"I have a wonderful idea for a new column," said Felicia. "I want to call it Heart of Dixie. I see it as a grapevine in print. I've got some sample copy here, Luke, so you can see what it would be like."

"If you two have your way you'll be turning the paper into some kind of true confessions mag," Kilroy complained. "Who wants to read gossip? Girls, that's all."

"I don't see what's wrong with girls," said Felicia. "They do make up fifty percent of the student body. They're readers, aren't they?"

"Don't think I don't appreciate the work you've done on this, Felicia," Luke said. "But I think we're forgetting here that a newspaper has to have balance." He leaned back precariously in his chair, his feet propped on the table at the front of the room. It said much for Happy's determination to maintain her position on the table that even the smell of Luke's disreputable Topsiders did not budge her from her perch. "Sure, Dr. Heartbreak is a hit," he went on, "but we don't want to just start running a bunch of Dr. Heartbreak clones. We want to develop the hard news angle, the feature angle, the sports coverage and so on. We want a well-balanced product."

"Right," said Kilroy. "That's just what I was saying."

"Maybe you could work with Reggie on sports, Kilroy," said Luke. "Give us a fresh point of view in that department."

Amazingly, Sam thought, things were going just as Luke had planned. It seemed that for the moment he was back in control of the paper. Anita was temporarily disheartened, Happy was lost in Rainbow Bright visions, and some staff members were actually working on stories and responding positively to their editor's suggestions. No wonder Luke was looking pleased with himself.

As for Sam, her pleasure at the improvement of the atmosphere at newspaper staff meetings was balanced somewhat with dismay at the way her free time had been rapidly eaten up by writing personal response letters. Sam had written so many Dr. Heartbreak letters that she had started thinking and even dreaming in them.

> Dear Dr. Heartbreak,
> I am the reasonably intelligent, reasonably attractive, reasonably mature author of one of the most popular pieces of journalism ever to grace the halls of Lee High, but nobody even knows it! Now I know how Superman must have felt when he was schlepping around as Clark Kent. Talk about unfair!
>
> Ghost Writer

Sam would have liked at least to get a little credit for all the work she was doing. But if she revealed her secret identity, not only would Pip, Marcy and Happy all be furious at her, but the column would go down the tubes. It was too bad that the only cure Dr. Heartbreak could offer for her own problems was the same that she offered so freely to others—patience and resignation.

When Sam settled down to work that night on her personal advice letters, Pip's words floated back to haunt her. "Haven't you noticed you always get the fuzzy end of the lollipop when that guy is around?"

"Sam!" her mother called. "Are you in there working again?" Her mother pushed open the door to the study, but Sam was able to hide most of the letters by slamming the desk drawer closed. She had worked out a system now so that only one or two letters were ever on the desk at a time and those could easily be concealed by careful placement of her arm or the sweater.

"Robin just called. She's coming home for the weekend. That's a nice surprise, isn't it?"

"That's a long way to come for just a weekend, all the way from Atlanta."

"I suppose she got one of those special low-cost flights. Let's try to get this place cleaned up a little bit, okay? Or do you plan for that navy sweater to stay on your father's desk permanently?"

"I'll clean up some in a minute. I need to work a while longer on this."

"Why don't you ever show your father and me some of your newspaper stories? Honestly, from the time you put in—"

"A lot of what I'm doing is just editing," Sam said quickly.

"Well, don't forget to get all that mess out of your bathroom—the wet panty hose and the sweater spread out on the towel, too. Robin's going to need someplace to put her things when she gets in tomorrow."

As soon as her mother closed the door Sam turned back to her letters. It was hard for her to get interested in mundane tasks like housecleaning when she was surrounded by letters containing people's most intimate secrets. The trust all these poor souls had in her was breathtaking. She had a position of heavy responsibility, giving out all that advice. Sophomores, juniors or seniors, intellectuals and Valley Girl types—they were all sending their problems to Dr. Heartbreak. Still, when she picked up the next envelope she caught her breath in surprise. It was from Marcy!

Dear Dr. Heartbreak,
Reading your letter to Toots in last week's *Traveler*, I was amazed at how well you understood me! It was as if you were inside my mind. Believe me there aren't too many people around who are sensitive to the problems of people with high grade point averages.

I thought your answer was perfect. I mean what you said about her not having to hide her light under a basket and yet being tactful about her achievements. I try very hard to do both of these things myself, but there are other things that are not so easy to handle. I refer, of course, to boys.

So far there is no romance in my life at all. I have been out on some dates, but always with the sort of guy who helps his father with his income tax. I would rather spend time with my friends, or even with a good book than spend any more evenings discussing the tax code.

I think the reason I do not get to know more interesting boys is that I don't have the time to hang around the mall. Also I do not giggle and act silly. Do you think this could be part of the problem? How can I meet the sort of boy who will sweep me off my feet and leave me breathless with passion? Please do not print this letter. I enclose $3, which I understand will cover the cost of a personal response.

Wistful

"Cripes!" breathed Sam. It just went to show that you could never be sure of everything that was going on in a person's mind, even if that person was your best friend. Sam stuck a sheet of paper into the typewriter.

Dear Wistful,
There is no easy answer to your problem, my dear child. Destiny takes a far larger hand in our lives than we would like to think. The *Titanic* and the iceberg, the spider and the fly—what brings these actors, large and small, together, but Fate. Trust me! Somewhere someone is looking for a girl with your special qualities of warmth and caring, and some starry and magical evening your lips will meet! Patience!

Sam felt she was getting to know Dr. Heartbreak very well indeed by now. He was exceedingly big on patience. Sam favored that tack because a person couldn't get in much hot water by being patient. Alerted by her mother to the dangers of giving out advice indiscriminately, Sam had made sure that Dr. Heartbreak took a cautious approach.

Next she polished off her standard answer to two girls who wanted to get boys to notice them.

Perhaps it is not meant to be. Only time will tell. Be your usual friendly self, my dear child, be confident of your attractions, show that you are enjoying life, that you are fun to be around and then—possess your soul in patience.

She toyed with the idea of getting this response mimeographed to save time. It was remarkable how many letters were on that one subject.

The next letter, however, was something out of the ordinary. The back of the envelope bore the unmistakable marks of having been stepped on by a muddy football cleat. Sam did not get many letters that had been spindled and mutilated, so she tore it open at once in case the condition of the envelope suggested an unusually distraught correspondent.

Dear Dr. Heartbreak,
I go out with the foxiest girl in school and when I say that, I'm not just whistling Dixie. She is built, man. I mean, this girl has a body that just doesn't quit. Also, she knows how to have a good time once she loosens up some. So why am I writing to you? It's this way—my girl keeps looking over my shoulder when she's talking to me. I know you're thinking that with a girl like this what are you doing talking, but I mean even if I'm just maybe filling her in on the football plays, just trying to get them straight in my mind, you know, she's always sneaking these looks over my shoulder. It's driving me nuts. What are you looking at? I ask her. Some guy you like better or something? No, she says. She is not looking for any other guy.

Give it to me straight, Doc. What do you think? Is this fox fixing to ditch me?

Sports Fan

Dear Sports Fan,
I speak to you as a woman, and perhaps that is

best, for only a woman can understand how for-
eign, how difficult to comprehend are the mys-
teries of football to one unversed in them.
Perhaps your beloved only needs a little instruc-
tion for her to be able to give you her undivided
attention. A little gentle joking about her inat-
tention, the thoughtful present of some helpful
reference book such as *The Powder Puff Guide
to Football* may be all that is needed to save your
romance. The girl assures you she is not looking
for any other young man. I suggest you take her
at her word, at least for now.

Of course you want a girl who can share in
your enthusiasms, appreciate your accomplish-
ments, and one who has eyes for you only. *This
is not too much to ask*. But bear in mind that like
success on the playing field, success in love cannot always be achieved without patient effort.

The door opened suddenly. "Sam? I thought you
were going to help out. Where are you? I'm going to
want to vacuum in there. Go up and start on your
room."

Sam ripped the letter to Sports Fan out of the typewriter. She did not think this cleaning frenzy of her
mother's was necessary. It wasn't as if Robin were
likely to go into Sam's bedroom and run her fingers
along the baseboards checking for dust. Instinct told
her, however, that pointing that out would be a mistake. Her mother sounded a bit on edge. Sam bounded
up out of the chair. "I'm going. I'm on my way. Is
anything wrong?"

"No, of course not. I just wonder why Robin is coming home so suddenly like this. You don't think she's lost her job, do you, Sam?"

"You think?" said Sam, brightening. "Neat!"

"Bite your tongue. If you'd ever had a taste of unemployment you wouldn't talk like that."

Sam ran upstairs. It was hard for her to treat Robin's job with any respect. Marketing can openers? For this, Robin had read Shakespeare and studied calculus? For this, she had won the senior drama prize and been elected editor of the annual?

Sam had not made any definite career plans herself, though a post as advice columnist was beginning to seem enticing. But she was positive it was not her destiny to spend her life dealing with can openers.

She threw open the door of her room and looked around, trying to decide where to begin. The trouble was, she had everything just the way she wanted it already. Her loafers were by the door where she could step into them at a dead run in the morning. Her nightgown was thrown over the foot of the bed, easily at hand. Her personal correspondence was stuffed in between the pink and the red bottles of fingernail polish, her favorite earrings, except for a few that had rolled under the bed, were spread out in front of the eye makeup, and her knee socks and argyles were hung on the knobs of the dresser. The system was the height of efficiency. If she started putting stuff away she wouldn't be able to find a thing for weeks.

Her mother stuck her head in the door. "This room looks like a cyclone hit it. It may come as a shock to you, sweetheart, but dresser drawers are not supposed to grow stalactites of knee socks. Get a move on. We don't have much time."

When Sam lifted a sock off a dresser knob to indicate her willingness to cooperate, her mother dashed away once more, calling as she went down the stairs, "As soon as you finish in there, come down to the living room and help me with the dusting."

Sam sighed. Maybe the best thing to do would be to stuff everything under the bed until Robin left. The dust ruffle would hide it.

She heard the doorbell ring downstairs and then heard her mother's voice pitched a quarter of an octave higher than usual. A few seconds later, Marcy appeared at Sam's bedroom, closing the door behind her.

"What's wrong with your mom? She's dusting down there. I don't think I've ever seen her dusting before."

Sam sighed. "She's always that way when we're going to have company. Not that this is really company, it's just Robin. But Mom's decided something's wrong with Robin, so that's added onto the usual company-is-coming craziness."

"What could be wrong with Robin?"

"Mom thinks maybe she's lost her job. You know Mom. Worry is her hobby." Sam pulled an empty shoe box out from under her bed and began stuffing socks into it.

"Aren't you even going to sort them out into pairs?" asked Marcy.

"Are you kidding? And have them multiplying in the night? Why don't you scoop up all those earrings over there and stuff them into the jewelry box?"

Marcy obediently opened the jewelry box. "If I did that, they'd get all tangled up in the necklaces."

"I know. Isn't this cleaning up ridiculous?" Sam sighed, kicking the shoe box back under the bed. "What's up?"

"I think I may be able to stick it out a while longer on newspaper staff. Things seem to have quieted down a little."

"It's the Dr. Heartbreak column," said Sam, flushing a little with pride. "It's distracted everybody."

"I guess. Do you think Luke seems happier now?"

"I suppose so," said Sam. She stuffed her nightgown into the drawer filled with her old sweatshirts, blue jeans, head scarves, stockings and underwear, then bumped her hip against it to close it.

"Don't you think it's time to clean out that drawer?"

"Not yet," said Sam.

"In this millenium, maybe?" inquired Marcy. As Sam began making the bed, Marcy sat down crosslegged on the floor where the china lamp on the dresser made highlights on her straight dark hair.

"Sam, don't you think it's about time Luke started thinking about something besides the paper?"

"Why do you say that? I can't believe you're worrying about Luke, Marcy. If you don't watch it you're going to get as bad as Mom. Next you'll start clipping out articles like 'The Hidden Symptoms of Heart Disease'."

"Well, I've just been wondering, that's all. Have you thought about how he hasn't been out with anybody since he and Jenny broke up last summer?"

"Who cares? Luke always has such awful girl-friends anyway. Remember Maggie?" Sam shuddered.

"His taste does seem to run to the bad, the blonde and the vicious, doesn't it? So you don't think it's a bad sign, then? You don't think that underneath that smile of his there's some deep hidden depression?"

"No, I don't."

"I guess it's just barely possible he's had a blinding flash of self-knowledge and realizing he always picks awful types he's decided to give up girls for his own good. What do you think?"

"I doubt it. Could you throw me that book?"

Marcy tossed her book, Sam checked the due date, then stuffed it under the bed with everything else.

"I wonder why he always picks such witches when he could have any girl in school?" asked Marcy, leaning her head back against the dresser.

"He couldn't have any girl, Marce. Some people like boys to be neat and clean. Some like really brainy types. Some like types who drive fancy cars. I mean, sure, we love Luke, but face it, he's got his little faults. What about those shoes of his? Yuck."

"Well, almost anybody, anyway. Anybody except the extremely picky. And another case of the same thing—look at Jim Shipman. He's gorgeous and he appears to be in full possession of his wits, and he picks Happy. Does this make sense? I tell you, Sam, I detect a pattern of mismanagement in people's romantic lives everywhere. Look around you."

"That's because they don't take Dr. Heartbreak's advice," said Sam.

"That must be it," said Marcy. When Sam swiftly glanced at Marcy, she was just opening her mouth and it looked as if she might be about to confess that she'd written to Dr. Heartbreak, but she closed it again and said nothing.

Sam sat down on the edge of the bed. "I think lots of people see ways they'd like to improve their love life, don't you?" she said encouragingly.

"I guess so," said Marcy.

"Like even with Pip and me there are a few things I'd like to change. Sometimes I'd like him to take me in his arms—"

"Get out of here, Sam. He's all over you already."

"And say something sweet," Sam finished with dignity. "I'd like him to say something romantic, something worth writing in my diary, you know?"

"Don't hold your breath," said Marcy.

The door opened and Sam's mother cast an eye around the room. "That's an improvement, Sam, but what about that candy paper in the corner? And your wastebasket is overflowing, too. Maybe you and Marcy had better visit sometime when we aren't as rushed."

"Marcy's helping me," said Sam.

Sam's mother departed, dragging the vacuum cleaner behind her. Sam could hear it going click-click against the floorboards of the hall.

Marcy scrambled up. "I'd better get out of your way, Sam."

"Look, I'm glad you're not quitting the staff, Marce. And don't worry about Luke. He's just concentrating on the newspaper. That's all. Just like you concentrate on grades. Actually, now that I think of it, I'm the only one of the three of us that isn't suffering from monomania.''

"Do you even know what monomania is, Sam?"

"Obsessed with one idea," said Sam triumphantly. "Hah! There are those who underrate my vocabulary, but they are so mistaken, benighted, misled."

Marcy smiled a little. "I'll have you know I do not suffer from monomania. I play the clarinet. I read the comics. I'm friends with you and Luke. You make me sound like that girl who wrote to Dr. Heartbreak."

Sam hopped up on the bed and stood holding a comb in the attitude of the Statue of Liberty. "Send your problems to Dr. Heartbreak. He has the answers!"

Marcy folded her arms and looked at Sam. "It's happened," she said flatly. "You're finally going around the bend."

Chapter Five

Saturday morning, Sam's entire family drove to the Raleigh-Durham airport to meet Robin's plane. Sam loved airports. It always seemed to her that anything was possible where baggage carts whizzed by and exotic destinations were posted behind every ticket counter.

At last they spotted Robin over at the luggage carousel. Her hair, which was naturally straight and blond like Sam's, had been permed in crimped little waves to her shoulders and she was wearing large dark glasses. Sam's spirits rose a little at these signs of big-city gloss. Robin was thinner than ever; her elbows were positively knobby. But when she whipped off her dark glasses and waved at them, Sam could see that her eyes were opened wide with excitement, and for a moment it seemed almost possible that something more interesting than an update on the can opener industry was in the offing. Perhaps Robin had been signed for a five-year film contract or was getting transferred to the island of Martinique.

"Mom, Dad, I'm getting married," squealed Robin, running toward them with mincing steps, her arms outstretched.

"You're getting married!" echoed her mother, her eyes glistening suddenly with tears.

"When do we get to meet the lucky young man?" said her father, sounding like a hearty-voiced imitation of himself.

"You're going to get married! That means we've got to put on a wedding!" said her mother, sounding a note of panic.

"Let's just get the luggage, Ginny, before you start planning the wedding. If we keep standing here, somebody's going to steal it." Sam's dad returned with Robin's overnight case. "You can't be too careful these days," he said.

"Oh, you're going to love Roger, Dad. You remember me telling you about Roger, don't you?"

"Roger?"

"He's the one that plays the violin," Sam's mother said. "Isn't he, Robin?"

"Of course. I've told you all about him, Dad. You must remember. He teaches music in the DeKalb County school system. I just know our children will be musical. We are always going to have fine music playing in the home—Mozart, Bach, Beethoven. Roger says those early years are so important."

Robin swung her carryall lightly at her side as she minced toward the automatic glass doors in the highest of heels. "I'm so happy. I want the wedding to be just perfect. I was thinking about it all the way on the flight up. It's too bad I look washed out in white. Maybe a very warm cream color. What do you think of ecru for the gown, Mom?''

To Sam, trailing behind the three of them, it seemed they had become caricatures of themselves—Mother of the Bride, Father of the Bride, and leading the pack, her bony arms swinging in excitement, the Bride.

What a letdown, Sam thought. No film contract. No Martinique. Sam counted on her fingers. Adding eight years to her own age, she quickly determined that Robin was twenty-four. Sam wanted to be older than that when she got married. Much older. Marriage was all very well for people like her parents who enjoyed nothing better than playing Scrabble in the evenings, but Sam hoped to see something of life and of assorted tropical islands before settling down to paying on a mortgage.

"When are we going to meet Roger's parents?" Sam heard her mother ask.

"Soon," said Robin. "Do you know they live only a half-hour's drive from here and Roger and I had to go all the way to Atlanta to find each other. Roger's telling them the news right now. I'm going to call him tonight and see if they can drive over together tomorrow. Sam, you look marvelous. I can't believe how you've grown up. Of course, you'll be one of the bridesmaids. I'm thinking of pink for the bridesmaids' dresses with bouquets of pink carnations. We'll have to get on the dresses right away. Roger says long engagements are for people who don't know their own minds. We thought maybe mid-December for the wedding."

"That's less than two months away!" said Sam's mother in alarm.

"Don't worry. Roger and I want it to be very simple. Just the friends we grew up with—"

"Two hundred," muttered her father.

"And of course Roger's people."

"Another two hundred," he said, beginning to sound depressed.

"A very very simple wedding," said Robin. "Roger loathes ostentation. But, of course, perfect in its way."

"Sam will be able to help out," said her father, glancing at her. Sam realized he thought she was feeling a little out of things and was trying to include her. Actually she did not feel left out. To the contrary, she had just had a glimmer of how this wedding was going to interfere in her life. Florists and caterers running in and out of the house, fittings for bridesmaids' dresses, consultations with the minister, messengers bringing wedding gifts, which had to be carefully recorded— something told her that with all this going on it was going to be very difficult to continue to operate Dr. Heartbreak's problem-solving business.

"Have you thought about eloping?" she asked Robin hopefully.

"Oh, Sam!" Robin laughed. "Naturally I want to get married in my old church, with Granny's veil, and something borrowed something blue and all that. Roger and I want to have a very traditional wedding. Roger says people don't pay enough attention to tradition these days. Mom, what do you think about those little paper napkins with 'Roger and Robin' on them? Do you think that would be tacky?"

Sam had the feeling her sister's mind had suddenly become petrified. It was hard to believe this was the girl who had aced Renaissance lit. The name Roger now seemed to form the major part of her vocabulary.

On the drive home, Robin and her mother were deep in discussion about the best place to have the reception and the burning question of rice versus birdseed.

"When Sue got married they had a birdseed-bagging party beforehand," Robin said, "which is one approach, but I think you can buy prefab birdseed, too, already stuffed in little plastic wedding bells."

"We have to decide on the reception, first," said her mother. "We're going to have to sit down with my address book tonight and make a list of all the out-of-town relatives."

"Or maybe Roger would rather have rice instead of birdseed. I'll have to ask him," said Robin thoughtfully. "After all, rice is more traditional."

It seemed to Sam that her own worries were more pressing than piddling matters such as rice versus birdseed. As soon as they got home she slipped away to her room and phoned Luke. "I need help on these personal response letters," she told him urgently. "I've got a really big stack of them, and you promised me you were going to help."

"The problem is, Sam, I'm not sure I can write letters that sound like Dr. Heartbreak. You've got his voice down pat now."

"Don't worry about that," said Sam. "This is no time to be picky. Robin is getting married and things are starting to fall apart around here. A lot of these letters take a standard response that you can just copy.

I'll give you a handful of 'what can I do to make him notice I'm alive' and another handful of 'the people at Lee are such snobs, how can I find personal happiness when I don't even own a Triumph.' Come over Monday night. Robin will be gone by then. You won't forget, now, will you?"

"Hey, didn't I say you could count on me?"

The next day, at Sunday dinner, while Sam was still in shock from Robin's announcement, the family entertained Roger and his parents. Roger was tall and skinny and had a prominent Adam's apple. Sam shook hands with him, all the time wondering how Robin could possibly think about marrying him. His hands were soft and moist.

Roger's parents rather reminded Sam of the Sprats in the nursery-rhyme book she had had as a kid. Roger's father was tall and skinny, but his mother was quite plump. She wore a dress with a draped bodice, a strand of pearls and matching pearl earrings.

"Roger was an Eagle Scout," Mrs. Odom was saying. "A model child in every way. People used to say to me, 'Myrtle, that child is too good to be true' because he was always such an angel, you see. He always got A's in deportment. He was a patrol boy, too, and paper boy of the year for the *Evening Star* for 1975."

"Now, Mother," said Mr. Odom. "He wasn't all that perfect."

"He was our baby, you see," Mrs. Odom confided. "People used to say to me, 'Myrtle, you'll spoil that boy rotten,' but I never worried about that. I just wanted him to be happy. The only thing I ever worried about was him finding a girl who was good enough for him. I suppose all mothers are like that.

But we are just in love with your Robin. Roger has done nothing but tell us how wonderful she is.''

After dinner, they all sat around in the living room. Roger and Robin sat by the fireplace holding hands, and Mrs. Odom sat on the couch between Sam's parents, showing them pictures of her grandchildren. A glance over her mother's shoulder told Sam all she needed to know. All the grandchildren had the Odom nose.

Dear Dr. Heartbreak,
My sister is about to make a dreadful mistake. She is marrying the Wrong Man. She has told my mother that he is everything she ever dreamed of in a husband. Is this evidence of insanity? If so, does it run in families? What can I do to stop her from making this terrible mistake?

Frightened

Sam knew what Dr. Heartbreak would say to that. He would say she couldn't do anything and he would be right. As Sam sat in the living room, looking at the Odoms, she had a very sobering thought. All of this romance that she was so fond of had a way of tending to end in marriage and the bringing of perfect strangers into the family. It was a dark side of the romance picture that she had never fully considered.

After the Odoms had cleared out, Sam called Pip and asked him to take her out for a drive. She had begun to feel if she stood around all evening listening to the maddening repetition of the name "Roger" she might just crack up.

"Oh, they can't be that bad," said Pip as they drove down Sunset Drive.

"They're awful," said Sam. "They call each other 'Mother' and 'Dad.' They chew breath mints. They show everybody pictures of their awful grandchildren."

"Well, she's not marrying them."

"You don't know much about relatives, if you think that. Why, they don't even live very far away. I'm beginning to get these awful premonitions. You know, like when Scrooge sees Christmas future and breaks out in a cold sweat? Besides, Roger's not so great himself. He has this high little laugh and when he sits down he sort of hoists up his pant legs. Also, he wears socks with little ducks on them."

"He probably has good qualities you can't see."

"I can't understand how Robin can go off and marry this perfect stranger!" cried Sam.

"She probably knows him a little better than you do."

"Okay, laugh at me. See how you like it when Terry brings home some stranger and makes him your brother-in-law."

"Never happen. My mother's family goes in for arranged marriages."

"You're not going to tell me your parents had an arranged marriage," she said, startled.

"Not really, actually, they eloped. My grandfather Byron was so mad he said he'd cut Dad off without a penny. My Posado grandparents insisted on a copy of the marriage license in Spanish and notarized by the Spanish consulate. I think they thought my father was trying to pull a fast one when the truth was Dad pulled off the elopement just to keep Grandfather Byron from interfering. Dad was afraid that if they had a traditional wedding, when they got to that part in the service about 'does anybody know any reason why this marriage cannot proceed,' his father would chime right in with ten or twelve objections. Now that was a good old-fashioned wedding. Everybody getting disinherited. Nobody speaking. They don't make them like that anymore."

Sam said gloomily, "I wish Robin would elope."

"Oh, cheer up, Sam. It won't be so bad."

Monday night, Luke came over as he had promised, to help with the Heartbreak letters.

"Look at the way they keep those cards and letters coming," he said, shuffling through the stack of envelopes. "They love us."

Sam handed Luke a small stack with a rubber band around it. "These are all 'he doesn't notice me letters.' My standard answer is right there next to the typewriter. You can get started on them."

Luke sat down in front of the typewriter. "Maybe I should jazz it up a little bit. Add a personal touch, you know?"

"No," said Sam firmly. "Just the stock response."

After Luke started typing, Sam took a handful of unopened envelopes over to her father's reclining chair to look through them. She saw that Sports Fan was already back in touch.

Dear Dr. Heartbreak,
Man, you could have knocked me down with a feather when I found out you were a girl! I was bowled right over. And this is what hit me. Wouldn't it be great if you and me could get together and talk? I'm not so good at getting stuff down on paper, as I guess you can tell.

You see, it's not just this business of my girl looking over my shoulder that's getting to me. There's other stuff, too. I guess I didn't mention that I'm the starting quarterback for our football team and when I look in the mirror it doesn't exactly break either. I been thinking about what you said about having a girl that appreciates me. What I'm getting at is I have the feeling this girl of mine is sort of along for the ride. Like she's more interested in my car than me. Hey, maybe I want something better, huh?

Sports Fan

Luke spun around in the desk chair. "How to make a boy notice you," he mused aloud. "Now I can think of a lot of ways to make a boy notice you. How about bikinis? How about see-through blouses? You've just skimmed along the surface of this subject, Sam."

"Just the stock answer, Luke. Our correspondents want romance; they don't want to be arrested."

"What's that letter you're reading?"

Sam quickly put it facedown on her lap. "That's confidential," she said.

"Ho, ho! Somebody we know, huh?"

She wondered what he would say if he knew she had Jim Shipman's letter in her lap. For after all, who else was the starting quarterback for the Rebels? To think that when she had seen Jim Shipman, tall handsome senior, pass by her in the hall she had never guessed that behind those chiseled features, that heavy jaw, was a tormented soul, a seeker after warmth and understanding.

"It's confidential."

"Oh, come on," he said, reaching for it.

Sam sat on the letter. "If you wrote to Dr. Heartbreak, would you want everybody reading your letter and laughing at it?"

"Me write to Dr. Heartbreak? You've got to be kidding. That would be the day."

"You would be surprised—" She hesitated.

Luke smiled. "Go ahead, Sam. What were you going to say?"

"I was only going to say that you would be surprised at how many hip, intelligent people write to Dr. Heartbreak, that's all. The world is indeed sadly short of warmth and understanding."

"You better watch it. You're starting to sound like Heartbreak."

"I could do worse. You would be astonished at how people respond to Dr. Heartbreak."

"I bet I would. Show me the letter."

"Sorry, we advice columnists have our code of ethics."

She was already sketching out an answer to Sports Fan in her mind. "Sure you understand... confidentiality... deepest interest in your problem."

She opened the next letter in the stack.

Dear Dr. Heartbreak,

I am seventeen and unofficially engaged. By unofficially I mean that if my parents had the slightest clue they would but totally annihilate me. In the first place, they cannot stand my boyfriend and in the second place, they want me to go to college. Because of this I wear my ring on a chain around my neck instead of on my finger, which my boyfriend does not like. My problem is that he is insanely jealous. If I just buy peanuts from the peanut vendor at the football game he tries to make out like I'm coming on to him. A peanut vendor! I mean, get serious! He says it's because I don't wear my ring, but that if I marry him right now he will not be jealous anymore. What do you think?

Doubtful

Luke had come over and was reading over Sam's shoulder. "There've got to be easier ways to get out of going to college," he said. "Drop him, Doubtful. Are all the letters that dippy?"

"Anybody can have problems with his love life, Luke. Even you."

"Ouch!" he yelped, grabbing his side and feigning a slide to the floor, which he artfully turned into sitting down on a hassock. "Okay, I've had my disasters in the past, I don't deny it. But no more. I'm giving up girls, burying myself in my work. All that wining and dining of little twits that turn out to be a royal pain in the neck—that's all behind me now. Old Doubtful should take a leaf out of my book."

"How many of those letters have you done?" asked Sam.

Luke glanced over his shoulder. "Two."

"Back to work, slave. Two is a mere drop in the bucket when you're dealing with Dr. Heartbreak's mail."

Pip did not usually drop in to see Sam without calling first. But he kept thinking about how upset she'd been about her prospective new in-laws and when he found himself going past her house on his way to the library, he decided to forget the library and stop by. Maybe he could cheer her up.

As he pulled up to the big old Victorian house on Mulberry Street, he saw Luke walking down the porch steps. Even in the sickly yellow glow cast by the porch light, Pip could make out the distinctive pale gleam of Luke's hair. To cinch the identification, he saw Luke's old green Pontiac parked illegally right next to the fire hydrant.

Pip slowed his car to a crawl because he didn't want to step out of it only to run right into Luke. He waited until Luke got in his car and roared off. Then he drew his Mercedes up into the driveway and got out. It was not that he was jealous, he told himself, as his footsteps sounded on the wood of the porch steps, but just the sight of Luke could spoil his whole evening. He couldn't stand the guy. Irresponsible. Heartless. A lot of smarmy charm. You couldn't tell Sam that, though.

Sam answered the doorbell. She was wearing blue jeans and an old sweatshirt and had a smudge of ink on her nose. Pip could feel himself softening. He loved looking at Sam. He could do it all day, and he couldn't have cared less what she was wearing, but part of his mind was relieved to note that she was not dressed like a girl expecting a boy that was anything special to her.

"Pip! Gee, it's great to see you. Come on in. Nothing's wrong is it?"

"Nope." He smiled and touched her nose. "You've got ink on you."

She energetically scrubbed at her nose with the sleeve of her sweatshirt until it was pink. He put his arm around her and drew her close to him until he could feel her breath tickling his neck.

"Pip!" she protested, squirming, but looking pleased. "Come on in. I'll fix you some cocoa or something. Mom! Pip's here."

"Hello, Pip," Sam's mother called, sticking her head out of the kitchen. "I'm on the phone to a caterer right now. I'll be off in a minute."

"Hi, Mrs. Morrison."

Sam's mother flashed him a smile and disappeared again.

"Looks like I just missed Luke," Pip said. "I saw him driving off."

Sam blushed. "We were working together. On the newspaper."

With a sinking feeling, Pip realized he had been wrong about not being jealous. He was jealous all right, who was he kidding? And why did Sam have to look guilty like that, just when he was feeling so good?

"Is everything okay?" Sam asked again anxiously.

Pip squeezed her. "Sure," he said. "Everything's fine. I knew you were feeling a little low, and I thought I'd come over and try to cheer you up."

"That was so sweet," she said. What was the matter with him? Pip thought unhappily. He might not be as good-looking as Luke, but he was taller, he was richer, he was brighter, he had never gotten suspended from school. And on top of that he was honest, trustworthy and absolutely nuts about Sam.

What was it going to take to make him feel okay? He wondered if it would be better if he had grown up in Fenterville and known everybody since the year one like Sam had. There was no denying that he sometimes felt a little out of it when Sam and her friends started doing the Three Musketeers bit.

"Aren't you spending an awful lot of time working on that paper?" he said. "I thought you people had more staff than you could use these days."

"I'm doing a lot of editing," Sam said. "Helping Luke out." Even in the dimly lit living room, Pip could see color rising to her face.

She turned away from him and went over to the dying fire. She threw another log on it and a shower of sparks flew up. "I'll hold off on fixing the cocoa until Mom gets off the phone in there," she said. "This wedding is taking over our lives. Last week we all still had personal identities. Now we're just the bride's family. It's like one of those science-fiction films where everybody's just innocently mowing the lawn and washing the windows and then this flying saucer lands one night and suddenly everybody's eyes turn Day-glo green and they start acting funny. My sister and my parents are possessed by the bridal industry. No kidding."

Pip sat down in the easy chair next to the fire and concentrated on not asking any more questions about Luke. Fruitcake, the family beagle, nudged Pip's hand with his head and whimpered until Pip began scratching him behind the ears. Sam prodded the logs with the brass poker and a few flames leaped up. "Are you cold?" she asked, looking at him anxiously.

"I'm okay." Pip drew Fruitcake's long, silky ears through his fingers, and the beagle sat rapt in a look of idiotic enjoyment.

Sam laid down the poker and sat on Pip's lap, arranging herself comfortably with his arms at her waist. "Maybe I'd better breathe on you," she said. "To help warm you up." She took his free hand in hers and puffed on it. Pip had the uncomfortable feeling that he must be wearing a look of idiotic bliss that matched Fruitcake's.

Some lighter threads of Sam's hair, so close, now, to his eyes, seemed to glitter in the uncertain light cast by the fire, the same light that cast a pink halo on her face. Pip felt as if a warm spell were falling over him. He tightened his arms around her and drew her to him. "I'm warmer already," he murmured in her ear.

Everything had become clear to him now. Sam was the only warm thing going in this cold and nosy little town. He needed her so much that when he had seen Luke at the house something went a little bit wrong in his brain.

There was a creak as the kitchen door swung open. "Anyone want some cocoa?" called Mrs. Morrison.

As the two of them struggled up out of the soft easy chair, Pip was making the firm resolution not to let his imagination run away with him anymore. This jealousy was craziness, that was all.

Chapter Six

Dear Dr. Heartbreak,
I am the beautiful, intelligent, extremely mature girl who wrote to you a few weeks ago. I do not think you understood my letter. It is not friendship I am after, so your advice about "be a friend" does not apply. Recognition of my worth is what I want.

Never mind about that now, though. I have an urgent problem that falls right in your area of expertise. My boyfriend, the star quarterback, is going all hot and cold on me. First he complained I wasn't paying enough attention to him. Now I have the distinct feeling there is someone else. The competition for this boy is very stiff, and I don't want to take the risk of making him mad at me in case it is all my imagination. What should I do? This is important. I am including six dollars in the hope of an extra speedy answer. Send it Special Delivery.

Beauty

Dear Dr. Heartbreak,
Up till I started hearing from you, it never hit me that this thing with my girl was strictly physical. Don't get me wrong. Physical is okay. But like you say, that's not all there is.

If I could just talk to you one to one, I think it would help me get things together. The way I figure it you've got a soft voice and long white fingers with maybe lots of rings. I see you as a very classy type. I've always liked girls with class. But I guess from what you tell me that getting together is out of bounds so I'm sending three bucks for another one of those personal responses.

Sports Fan

Dear Dr. Heartbreak,
I understand perfectly that destiny takes a large hand in our affairs but isn't there something I could do to hurry it along a little? My best friend has been utterly swept off her feet by this tall, animallike guy who drives a fancy car and while he is most emphatically not my cup of tea, I can't help feeling that this swept-up sensation would be interesting at the very least.

Do you ever meet with your clients? I feel as if I would get a lot more out of a personal encounter. So much nuance is lost in a letter, don't you think?

Wistful

Dear Dr. Heartbreak,
I am in love with a beautiful woman. Although we are not in the habit of getting mushy I know in my heart

that she cares for me as much as I care for her. I can see it in her eyes when she looks at me.

My problem is that I am jealous, and it is poisoning my life. She has a friend, a boy, who is so good-looking that he could have stepped off of a greeting card. I saw him leaving her house last week, and though I believe her when she says they were only working together, I find myself thinking lately how much pleasure it would give me to stomp on his pretty face.

All my life I have been a person with mostly quiet, intellectual interests and maybe a little tennis now and then. I cannot deal with all this insane emotion. What shall I do?

Quiet Man

Sam sat in the recliner, with letters heaped carelessly around her and stared at the last letter. She turned the envelope over gingerly and checked the return address. It was Pip all right. Some obscure impulse made her raise the envelope and brush it against her lips. Pip really could come out with sweet things after all. But she had never imagined she would hear these things via a letter that scared her speechless.

Of course, there was nothing between her and Luke and never had been, but that didn't make Sam feel as secure as it should have. It struck her suddenly that something that existed purely in a person's imagination could be just as dangerous as something that was real. Dr. Heartbreak, for example, was imaginary and yet he was having a tremendous impact. It could work the same way with Pip's imaginings about her and Luke. When she read over Pip's letter she realized how vulnerable her situation was. What if somebody discovered this weakness of his and persuaded him there was something to it, somebody unscrupulous like Happy?

Once Sam's parents had driven her to Chapel Hill to see a production of Othello. Sam had thought Othello was an awful jerk to believe the lies Iago told him about Desdemona.

"Unrealistic," she had said when they were leaving afterward. But to her dismay, the play didn't seem all that unrealistic right at the moment. Scenes and lines from it had suddenly begun floating in her mind.

Sam looked at the letters spilled around her. Marcy was right. Everybody's romantic life was hopelessly mismanaged and Sam didn't feel capable of straightening it all out. She couldn't even quite figure out how to straighten out her own.

The door of the study flew open. "Sam, did Garden of Eden call with those quotes today?" asked her mother.

"I think I put them on top of the refrigerator."

"Put them on the bulletin board next time. If we don't get organized we are going to be in the soup. Do you know I have made four calls to that photographer? Sometimes I wonder if those people really want the job. Have you set up a time for your fitting with Miss Blitch?"

"All taken care of. Only Mom, there's just this one little thing. The Christmas dance is going to be the week before the wedding."

"What do you want me to do, Sam? If you want to go to that you are going to have to wear a dress you've already got, because this wedding is costing an arm and a leg and I cannot see laying out any more money right now."

"Okay."

"Are you running a fever or something," her mother said, putting her palm on Sam's forehead. "You don't feel hot, but you don't seem quite yourself, either. Take some vitamins. I can't afford to have you getting sick now, of all times."

Sam promised to take her vitamins. Once her mother left, she stared at Pip's letter for a long time. It was crucial that she give exactly the right answer. She couldn't make any mistakes. Also, she wanted to be careful not to sound too come-onish. The very last thing she wanted was for Pip to start getting a crush on Dr. Heartbreak the way so many of her other correspondents seemed to be doing. She thought a long time before she pulled up a chair and sat down at the typewriter.

Dear Quiet Man,
How hard it is for us to feel that we are worthy of love and yet how essential to our peace of mind! You say you know your affection is returned, and I am certain that is true.

I sense that you are a person of unusual determination. Can you not resolve to put these wayward thoughts out of your mind? When you find yourself thinking jealous or angry thoughts, do something at once to banish them. A brisk walk might be helpful, or a phone call to your beloved. Let me know how you are getting along. I am more than usually interested.

Sam folded the paper and put it in the self-addressed, stamped envelope he had sent her. She had her fingers crossed so hard her rings were biting into the flesh.

Feeling drained, she stuffed all the rest of the letters in the drawer. Marcy would be home from work by now. Sam decided to pop over and say hello.

Marcy lived with her mother in a garage apartment where frilled curtains at the windows and a quilted country style wreath on the door made a valiant effort to distract attention from the rickety construction and the aged paint job. Marcy's mother had, since her divorce, been trying to train herself as an accountant in the hope of advancing in her work, which meant she was out most evenings at classes.

This place is depressing, Sam thought as she stood in the fading light waiting for Marcy to come to the door. Peeking through the quilted wreath, she could see the couch inside with the coverlet spread over it to hide the worn upholstery and Marcy's school books spilled over it.

"Let's go to Burger King for supper," she said, as soon as Marcy opened the door. "My treat. I need some cheering up."

"Join the club," said Marcy, reaching for her jacket. "Mom's at class. I was just going to heat up a can of soup. Your folks aren't expecting you home for dinner?"

"Dinner? I do sort of remember having a real dinner once upon a time, but since Mom and Robin started planning the wedding all we get is a choice between Morton's and Stouffer's."

Someone was burning leaves, and the smoke was blowing in their direction, but as the two girls got into Sam's car, Sam thought she could still catch a faint smell of gasoline. She hoped her old car was not about to break down again. If her mother didn't want to lay out the money for a new dress, she wasn't going to want to lay out the money for a new carburetor, either.

"What are you depressed about?" asked Marcy.

"Pip is jealous of Luke. Can you believe that?"

"That seems funny. What exactly did he say?"

"He didn't exactly say anything, but I *sense* it," Sam said carefully. "He asks me questions, like why is Luke over at the house?"

"And why is Luke over at the house?" Marcy asked.

"Oh, just picking up things for the newspaper and whatever."

Marcy got in the car. "Do you read that Dr. Heartbreak column, Sam?"

"Now and then. I mean, I think I've read, well, most of them, probably." Sam hoped she was not blushing.

"Do you remember Dr. Heartbreak's advice to Doubtful? Doubtful was the one whose boyfriend was jealous of the peanut vendor. Dump him, said Dr. Heartbreak!"

"Dump him? She said that?"

"Dr. Heartbreak is a boy, Sam," said Marcy, giving her an odd look.

"Do you think so?" Sam gulped. "I don't know why but I thought maybe it was written by a girl. Why not? Doctors can be male or female, you know."

"What makes you think it's written by a girl?"

Sam thought fast. "I guess because it's so sympathetic."

"I'm sure it's a boy," said Marcy.

"Whoever it is I think that was very dumb advice he or she gave to Doubtful. Besides it's not the same kind of thing at all. I'm not doubtful at all. I adore Pip."

Marcy shrugged.

Sam steered into the Burger King parking lot and they piled out. Light spilled into the parking lot from the big windows and Sam could see her breath in the cold air. Her ears were so cold they hurt. She thrust her hands deeply in the pockets of her jacket and hurried inside.

The place was practically deserted, and they were able to go straight up to the counter and give their orders.

"I love hamburgers," Sam told Marcy as they waited. "I do not like weddings, the color pink, turnips or jealousy. Why are people's lives so hard to manage?"

"Don't ask me. I'm not Dr. Heartbreak."

Sam blinked, but when she looked at Marcy searchingly she saw no sign that she was hinting at anything.

"Chip Eagleton asked me to the Christmas dance," Marcy said.

"That's nice," said Sam absently.

"I told him no. I'm not going with Chip. I'm going to dish out punch instead."

Their order appeared, they took their trays to a table and Sam began unwrapping her burger.

"Isn't Chip going to be pretty insulted when he finds out you'd rather dish out punch than go with him?"

"I don't care, Sam. His ears stick out."

"But what does that matter? Looks aren't that important."

"They're important to me. If you'd spent your whole life getting paired up with guys who speak in polysyllables you'd know what I mean. I'm tired of people thinking I'm going to like somebody just because he makes good grades. I like good looks, I like charm, I like passion. Three cheers for the things that aren't supposed to matter! They matter to me!"

"You sound kind of giddy," Sam said, looking at her with concern. "Have you been working too hard?"

"Of course, I have been working too hard. I only wish I were giddy. I'm entitled." Marcy stuck her spoon in the ice cream and left it there. "Actually, Sam, I am thinking of having a little adventure. Don't go spreading it around, but I have been writing to Dr. Heartbreak."

"You have?"

"Why not? We know he's somebody our age but in another town, right? I figure he's probably right in this state because if he were syndicated all over the country he would probably cost too much for Luke to pick up the tab, and he told me himself he was paying it out of his own pocket and it wasn't that much. So I figured, what the heck. I'm working now on getting together with him."

Sam choked on her milk shake. "Are you telling me you've got a date with Dr. Heartbreak?"

"Not yet. But I'm sort of moving in that direction. He's been extremely friendly. I sense that we're on the same wavelength. I'm sure there's something there."

"But Marce, I thought you said looks were important. For all you know Dr. Heartbreak's ears stick out even more than Chip's."

"No, I'm sure they don't stick out. I can almost see him. I imagine his voice is sort of deep and understanding and that he has these cool, clear eyes. Blue. Yes, the more I think about it the more sure I am they must be blue."

A cold draft hit Sam in the back of the neck, and she turned to see Jim Shipman coming in with Happy.

"Speaking of good-looking," said Marcy. "Here comes a prime example of same."

Sam could feel her ears burning as she looked at Jim. Of course, there was no earthly way for him to know she was Dr. Heartbreak, she reminded herself, but she quickly averted her face just the same.

A second later she could feel him looming over her and she was almost afraid to look up.

"Hello, there," said Happy sweetly. "Spending a night out with the girls? Do you two know Jim? Jim, this is Marcy and Sam, a couple of the kids who help me out on newspaper staff."

Sam saw that Happy's hand rested on one of Jim's broad shoulders, as if they were about to waltz around the restaurant.

"Hi, there," Jim said, looking a little embarrassed.

"When Jim gets out of football practice he's just ravenous," Happy explained. "So sometimes we come by here to get him six or eight burgers to tide him over until dinner. Did you see our game against Brixton? Jim was just amazing." Happy gazed up at his rugged profile with a look of open adoration. Sam was interested to see that Happy was putting into practice Dr. Heartbreak's advice to "let him know how much you care about him."

"I'm afraid I missed that game," Marcy was saying.

"Marcy is such a grind," said Happy, with a little tinkling laugh. "It's work, work, work with her all the time. I hate to think of what she thinks of all of us who just wing it."

"I have to study a lot, too," Jim said to Marcy sympathetically.

Marcy's nostrils flared slightly as she caught her breath, and for a moment Sam was afraid she was going to let loose a blast of eloquence demonstrating that she was not the village idiot, but to her relief, Jim spoke first.

"Happy's always telling me about the newspaper. Looks like you keep her pretty busy over there, running everything."

"So true," said Marcy, her attractive contralto hinting at quantities of barely suppressed emotion. "I don't know what we would do without Happy, do you, Sam? So helpful, right there in any pinch, a real team player. Often I say to myself 'We just don't give that girl enough credit.' Think of what she's *done* for us. Remember when she started up a competing paper, Sam?"

"We'd be *delighted* to hear you tell us the entire history of the *Traveler*, Marcy," said Happy, "but Jim and I have to *rush* off now. I know he's simply starving." She smiled at them. "He needs *so* many calories."

"Nice meeting you," Jim called as Happy steered him toward the counter.

"That queen of the universe act of hers," muttered Marcy, "drives me crazy. Did you get that stuff about how we're helping her out at the paper, hah! I'd like to help her out, all right. And the way she oozes phoniness! I'm surprised he doesn't see right through her.''

"Maybe he does," Sam said. She opened her hamburger and carefully examined the pickle.

Marcy was still watching Happy and Jim at the counter. "He's putting in his order. What do you want to bet he's asking for his hamburgers raw?''

"I thought you sort of liked him," said Sam.

"I think he's incredible," said Marcy. "Those broad shoulders, the narrow hips, the jaw like a bulldozer. I tell you Sam, I am getting in touch with primitive parts of myself that I never knew I had. There's a whole world out there beyond *Reader's Guide to Periodicals*. Life in the rough. That's what I need. I've only started realizing it lately.''

"You're working too hard.''

"Would you quit saying that? You sound like a broken record.'' Marcy spooned up some ice cream. "When I consider my state of mind and analyze it, I can trace the origins of this sudden realization that I was missing out on life. I think it began when you started going out with Pip. I began to feel as if you had graduated and left me behind. You were into something really special while I was still acting out this empty charade with boys who reminded me of damp Kleenexes.''

"Oh, Marce, you just haven't found the right boy for you, yet. That's all.''

"And then next there's this Dr. Heartbreak column suddenly coming out every week full of love, love, love. All those letters are written by high school kids just like you and me, Sam, and they're going through all kinds of anguish and despair, all sorts of terrible love situations. I ask myself, what's wrong with me. Why am I missing out on all that fun?'' She prodded her melting milk shake with her spoon.

"You don't think you could find what you're looking for with Chip Eagleton?" suggested Sam. "He's a very nice boy."

"Chip Eagleton does not light my fire," Marcy said positively.

Sam was beginning to be aware of a dreadful temptation. Here was Marcy, a sensitive, intelligent girl with a lot of depth who was getting a crush on Dr. Heartbreak. And in a booth on the other side of the restaurant was Jim Shipman, a gorgeous hunk who seemed to fit her bill in every particular way and who happened, coincidentally, to be looking for a sensitive, intelligent girl with a lot of depth. He also had a crush on Dr. Heartbreak. There was a beautiful symmetry there that was hard for Sam to ignore. She wondered what could be done with it. She was already getting an idea, but a lot of details needed working out.

Suddenly Sam heard a drumming sound on the big window across the aisle from them, and she looked up to see Luke waving both arms at them and grinning insanely, his nose pressed against the window.

"It's Luke!" cried Marcy in delight. "The gang's all here!"

A minute later he had slid into a seat at their little table and Marcy was smiling at him. "You looked utterly insane out there. What was that, a war dance or something?"

He began stuffing two of Marcy's french fries into his mouth. "Ancient Polynesian fertility dance."

"What is this?" said Sam. "Does everybody around here have sex on the brain or something?"

"It's that Dr. Heartbreak column," said Luke, winking at her. "It's corrupting the morals of the young."

"Isn't that odd you should mention it?" said Marcy. "Sam and I were just this minute talking about that column."

"What a coincidence!" said Luke. "Now that's really amazing."

Sam took out three dollar bills and laid them pointedly before him. "Go buy your own french fries, Luke. My treat."

Luke held them up as if checking to see if they were counterfeit. "The girl is flush. Do you have a part-time job or anything like that, Samantha?"

Sam shot him a look that said "get lost and shut up." She realized that the more people who wrote to her and confided their secrets, then the more people who would be livid if her identity were revealed. She had an ever increasing stake in secrecy. Unfortunately, Luke, who ate and drank risk as if it were a chocolate milk shake, was becoming increasingly a liability in their partnership.

As soon as he had gone up to the counter, Marcy leaned over and whispered, "Don't mention to Luke that I've written to Dr. Heartbreak, Sam, okay?"

"Oh, sure," said Sam. "Don't worry." She could have added that confidentiality was practically her middle name these days. She was currently a storehouse of half the secrets at Lee High.

A few minutes later, Luke slid back into his seat and dumped some fries out on his tray. "All together now," he said softly, lifting his finger to direct them, "hail, hail, the gang's all here!" They had whispered the entire chorus of the song in unison and wound up with their secret handshake.

"We get quieter and quieter," Marcy said. "I expect it's finally going to get so quiet, so vestigial, that we're going to be down to one softly muttered 'hail.' "

"Look, we can sing a loud, rousing chorus if you like," said Luke. "All together now—"

"No, no! Stop him, Sam. Pour your drink on his head or something."

"It will be a pleasure," said Sam grimly.

"I like that," he said. "Try to bring a little fun into your friends' drab lives and this is the thanks you get. Will you get a load of Jim Shipman over there with Happy?"

"Disgusting, isn't it?" said Marcy. "Look how she's all over him. You should have seen them when school was just starting. It was like watching *Wild Kingdom* with the tiger stalking ever closer to the tethered goat."

"Then flash to the smile on the face of the tiger," said Luke. "Well, I'm not complaining. As long as Happy's queening it over the football team, maybe she'll be too busy to cause any more trouble with the newspaper staff."

Sam was suddenly thoughtful. Luke had brought up a question she hadn't considered. If Dr. Heartbreak somehow managed to get Jim away from Happy, would Happy take out her frustrations on the newspaper? As Dr. Heartbreak, she had to consider not just Marcy's happiness, but the big picture. For the first time in her life, Sam felt a pang of sympathy for the organizational difficulties God must face.

Chapter Seven

Transference is the word you're trying to think of, Sam," said her mother as she wiped a dish dry. "That's when a therapy patient gets a crush on the therapist. I don't really understand all the ins and outs of it. Why don't you see if it's in the encyclopedia? Or I could see if someone at work has a book you could borrow. How did you get interested in transference? Is this for a report?"

"It's that Dr. Heartbreak column," explained Sam. "A couple of the kids I know are getting crushes on Heartbreak. They want to turn a few letters into a relationship."

"I think the theory behind transference is that the person is recreating other important relationships in his life, projecting them onto this vaguely known, sympathetic person. Do you see what I mean? I'll really have to get a book from Myra, Sam. This isn't my field at all."

"But that's exactly the way it is, Mom! Just what you said. They sort of make up someone and decide that's what Dr. Heartbreak is like. What I want to know is, is that bad or good?"

"You'd have to ask Myra. Who is it that has these crushes? Anyone I know?"

"Marcy, for one. Only don't tell anybody, because she's embarrassed about it. I would be, too. Imagine getting a crush on somebody you don't even know!"

"I'm afraid poor Marcy is rather lonely," said Sam's mother. "Sarah does the best she can, of course, but all those night classes! Well, it's a tough situation."

Sam felt a pang of guilt that she was not spending more time with Marcy. "She just wants a boyfriend," she said, vigorously wiping a dish.

"It is such a mistake to leap into these premature emotional involvements when all a person needs is a little closeness." Her mother sighed.

That was so typical of her mother, Sam thought impatiently. Where other people saw "boyfriend," her mother saw "premature emotional entanglement." Maybe it was because she was a social worker, always looking on the seamy side of life. Marcy's difficulty seemed simple enough to Sam. As the brainiest, hardest-working girl at Lee High, she had an image problem. When people threw a wild party, Marcy was the last person they thought to invite. When a boy started thinking of getting off alone with a girl in some dark secluded spot, Marcy's name was the last one to occur to him. Marcy was so serious, so dedicated, no one ever guessed she craved romance. Even Sam, her best friend, had been surprised to learn she was scheming to meet Dr. Heartbreak. A person didn't connect the intellectual Marcy with flaky ideas like that.

"If you can finish up in here for me, Sam, I need to get down to those reports," said her mother. "I had to take two hours for lunch in order to go traipsing around to florists today, and I'm unbelievably behind. I've got stacks of things in there I need to work on."

Sam willingly agreed to finish up the dishes. Actually she was glad to have some quiet time to think. She kept wondering if it were possible to work out a foolproof, no-risk solution to Marcy's problem. Surely, there must be a way. After all, she was producing solutions to other people's problems every day as Dr. Heartbreak. She ought to be able to help her own best friend.

For now, her plan was just to keep writing to Jim and Marcy to keep them on the hook. When she next wrote to Wistful and Sports Fan she had decided she was going to waive her three-dollar fee. She was surprised she hadn't thought of that before. It would encourage them and at the same time would be perfectly safe, committing her to nothing.

Just as Sam was stacking the last dish, the phone in the kitchen rang.

"Sam? It's Luke. I have some free time. Want me to come over and hack out a few of those letters for you?"

"No! Don't do that!"

"What's going on with you? You were begging me to do it the other day."

Sam swallowed. "I just don't think you need to come over. It's too risky." The idea that Pip might see Luke hanging around the house gave her chills. On the other hand, she certainly did need help with those letters. "I'll tell you what," she said, finally. "I'll drop off a bunch of the ones that can be answered with form letters in your locker at school."

"Don't you think it's going to be pretty obvious what's going on if somebody sees you dumping a bunch of letters in my locker?"

"Of course, I'll wait until nobody's around. You'd better give me your combination."

"You don't need the combination. I don't lock it."

"Luke, if I'm going to dump the letters in there, you've *got* to lock it."

"Okay, I'll lock it." She could almost hear the shrug in his voice.

"Do you want to see me tarred and feathered and ridden out of town on a rail?" she asked him, her voice strained.

"Keep your shirt on, Sam. I said I'd lock it, didn't I?"

"All right, then."

She wrote down the combination as he gave it to her. But, knowing Luke, she felt she'd have to go by his locker three times a day just to make sure he had locked the thing. She must have been out of her mind to enter into a risky partnership with him of all people.

"You worry too much," he said. "This stuff is going like gangbusters, isn't it?"

"Dr. Heartbreak does seem to be a success," Sam admitted.

"Don't go making yourself crazy, then. Enjoy."

After she hung up, she reflected that one of the most annoying things about Luke was that he could never see what the problem was. There was such a thing as being too laid-back.

She went into the study and began going methodically through the Heartbreak letters, tossing the ones that could be answered with form letters into a separate stack for Luke. Although she had been surprised by the number of people who had written to Dr. Heartbreak, she realized that the one letter she kept expecting had not arrived. She had yet to hear from Anita Jolley.

Anita, she reasoned, was entirely a mess in every way—her grooming, her personal relationships, her attitude. What would be more natural than that she should seek help from Dr. Heartbreak? Sam fairly itched to get her hands on the girl, the ultimate challenge to Dr. Heartbreak's counseling skills. She had even looked up Anita's address in the phone book so as to be alerted at once if the right envelope came through her hands. Not that it was necessary. She was sure she would sense an Anita envelope with her fingertips on account of it's having a certain grungy, tough quality. An Anita envelope, Sam thought, would be akin to a rhinoceros pelt that had been improperly cured. But as Sam leafed expectantly through the stack of letters, there was no sign that Anita was ready to turn her troubles over to Dr. Heartbreak.

Sports Fan, on the other hand, was already back in touch.

Dear Dr. Heartbreak,
The more I write to you the more I get the feeling there's something there, you now what I mean?

Something real big. I keep going out with this other girl, but all the time I have this feeling I'm just going through the motions, like when you're 52-0 in the last ten seconds of the game. I say you and me should get together and see if any sparks fly. I'm sending the usual three bucks. Let me know pretty soon about this.

Sports Fan

Marcy, too, was in touch.

Dear Dr. Heartbreak,
I can't tell you how much I admire your clear, incisive and wise answers to the troubled souls who write to you. You are indeed a guide, philosopher and friend.

From what you say, it seems so clear that we have much in common. Perhaps you feel, as I do, that it would be fascinating to meet and explore these shared interests. Do you know the Philatelic Society Stamp Shop in Raleigh? What a thrill it would be to me, as I go in there some Saturday, to feel that I might meet you there!

Wistful

Sam began typing out replies to these letters. "Sense a deep bond of sympathy... Do me the favor of not enclosing the three dollars henceforth...two hearts that beat as one...grieved that considerations of confidentiality prevent—"

"Sam!" called her mother. "Phone for you. It's Pip."

Sam tore the sheet she was working on out of the typewriter, stashed it in the drawer and dashed out of the study. "I'll take it upstairs," she yelled. She ran up to her room, grabbed the phone.

"Sam?" said Pip's voice. "Hey, I'm not calling about anything in particular. I just wanted to hear your voice."

Pip's words struck sudden fear into Sam's heart. Hadn't she told him, when he was feeling doubts, to call up his beloved?

"Oh, I'm so glad you did call," she said, her voice quavering a little. "I love to hear your voice, too."

"You sound funny, Sam. Is anybody, uh, is anybody over there or anything?"

"No. Nobody's here at all. I'm just a little out of breath because I ran all the way upstairs to the phone, that's all." She threw herself down on her bed. It was so hard to talk on the phone, she thought. Feelings seemed to get lost somewhere along the long telephone wires. "Oh, Pip, I wish you were here," she burst out.

"I'll come right over," he said.

After he hung up, Sam pulled a pillow over her head and groaned. Why did she say she wanted him to come over? She hadn't even finished the two letters to Wistful and Sports Fan. And what with studying for the Wednesday chemistry test she was getting further and further behind.

Dear Dr. Heartbreak,
I did not realize that being the fount of all wisdom was going to turn out to be such a strain. Can you tell me the secret to carrying on both a life and a career?

                                     One Who Needs to Know

Sam closed her eyes. She had not slept very well the night before. She had been disturbed by a dream in which Happy had been sitting up high on a giant mushroom. Happy had been wearing horn-rim glasses and smoking a hookah and kept looking down on Sam and asking in that snooty voice of hers, *"Who* are *you*?" The words had chilled Sam. Did Happy know Dr. Heartbreak's secret identity? Pip was in the dream somehow, too, but Sam had not been able to find him. He was lost or Happy was hiding him. That part was a little unclear. Sam had woken up at 3 a.m. in a cold sweat, wondering if microwaved frozen lasagna could possibly give a person nightmares.

The sound of the doorbell made her eyes fly open, and she realized she had been so tired she had fallen asleep for a moment. This time she couldn't remember her dream but it had something to do with losing Pip and she got up with a faint feeling of dread. Slipping on her shoes, she hurried downstairs.

Pip was at the door. Sam threw her arms around him and buried her nose in his rough red sweater.

"Hello!" he said, stroking her hair. She looked up to see that his eyes were crinkling in laughter. He did not look a bit like Othello, which was reassuring under the circumstances.

"I've been having bad dreams," she said.

"Hey, it's okay. You're awake now."

"Pip!" Sam's mother said, appearing at the door of the living room. "I thought I heard you. Come in here and give us an unbiased opinion about this."

Wedding presents in white boxes stood in piles all over, and the floor was littered with tissue paper and excelsior. Several index files spilled their contents over the closed top of the grand piano. It seemed to Sam that the wedding was sucking up their entire house as surely as if it had been the Giant Blob on a rampage.

Her parents were sitting on the couch looking at glossy photographs spread out on the coffee table. Beside the couch, Fruitcake was burrowing noisily into a large mass of crumpled tissue paper. He dug in it with much rustling, then circled around as if about to bed down in a pile of leaves.

"You have to imagine this a little bit more on the pink side," Sam's mother explained to Pip, indicating an 8 by 10 photograph of a nave featuring exposed rafters and maroon walls.

"It's that fast film I had to use," her father added. "It picks up colors better in the blue range."

"Try to envision pink carnations here and here," said Sam's mother, whipping out squares of paper cut out of a seed catalog and slapping them on top of the glossy. "Got that? Next picture white chrysanthemums, the big spidery ones. Which is better?"

"Both look fine to me," said Pip. Sam could feel Pip's hand warm and strong at her waist.

"I hate pink," said Sam. "It reminds me of Pepto Bismol."

"When you get married you can have white or purple or whatever you want," said her mother. "But for now, let's just worry about this wedding, okay?"

"I'm not going to get married until I'm quite old," said Sam. "Thirty, at least."

"You think?" said Pip, his eyes widening a little. He lifted a strand of her hair absently with his finger and smiled at her.

"And then I'm going to elope," Sam said. "I think all this stuff is absolutely disgusting. An orgy of sentimentalism and commercialism, that's what it is."

"You can see why we need an impartial opinion," said Sam's dad dryly.

"What does Robin say about the colors?" Pip asked.

"Robin can't make up her mind," said Sam's father. "Also, as I remind myself daily, Robin is not paying for these ridiculously expensive flowers."

"I think either pink or white would be fine," said Pip. "Or maybe a mix of pink and white."

"That's a possibility we haven't thought about," said Mrs. Morrison, looking startled. "Pink and white. Maybe we have something there."

Sam took a step backward and Pip, taking his cue from her, turned to go.

"Don't you two want to sit in here by the fire?" asked Sam's mother.

"No, we want to go out on the front porch," Sam replied.

"It's pretty cold out there," Sam's mother said.

"We like the front porch. I'll get my jacket."

Sam had to run upstairs for her jacket and when she came down with it, Pip was waiting for her at the foot of the stairs, leaning against an outstretched arm and looking out the window. She tiptoed up behind him, noticing as she drew near the faint line of downy, dark hair that ran down his neck to meet the scarlet splash of his sweater. "Boo!" she said, grabbing at his ribs. He turned swiftly and, looking down at her, grinned.

"Is it really cold out there?" she asked.

"Freezing," he said soberly. "I'm afraid we can't go on meeting like this."

"Not unless we get battery-powered socks, anyway," she agreed.

They sat on the porch swing in the dark, listening to its monotonous creaking. Pip clasped both of Sam's hands inside his own and nuzzled her cheek.

"Don't you think all that wedding stuff is disgusting?" she said, shivering a little. "Who cares what color the stupid flowers are? You'd think they were laying ground plans for the creation of the world. And get this, Robin is going to carry a bouquet with ivy in it that's rooted from the ivy that was in mother's bridal bouquet, she's going to wear Granny's veil and she's going to have this friend of hers play 'I Love You Truly' on the guitar. Can you believe that? 'I Love You Truly.' I am not putting you on."

"Heck, Sam, I thought that was the kind of thing you were crazy about. Hearts and flowers. Violins."

"This is different," Sam said stubbornly. "This is not romantic, this is just plain embarrassing."

"I think it's probably one of those things that looks different depending on whether it's happening to you or somebody else—like being scared out of your mind, or fighting mad. It all seems stupid to you because you don't like this guy she's marrying, but if you were the one getting married it would look different." She saw the flash of his white teeth as he smiled. "At least I hope so," he said.

She realized he was probably right. Pip, in his calm, reasonable way, had a habit of being right.

Dear Dr. Heartbreak,
I am immature and selfish and can't seem to put myself in the place of others. It's not that I don't know better because, as you know yourself, when I am being *you* I am amazingly wise. It's just that real life is different. In real life, I am afraid. I

have bad dreams. Change frightens me.

"Are you still asleep or something, Sam? Didn't you hear me?" Pip was saying.

Sam blinked. "I'm sorry. I guess I blacked out for a while. The way things are falling apart around here I have just got to get more sleep."

"I said I think I love you."

"Oh, no!"

"I don't think it's that bad," he said, taken aback.

"But I missed it!" Sam wailed. "Dumb, dumb, me, I missed it."

"Hey, calm down. If everything goes right I might say it again sometime."

She threw her arms around him and squeezed hard. "I don't ever want you to go away," she said.

"Not much danger of that," he said. He let his fingers run through her hair. "Oh, I love your hair."

Sam felt happiness washing over her in a tide. She had an almost bursting sense that the world was ripe with possibilities. Later she realized that it was at that moment she decided to go through with her plan to get Marcy and Jim Shipman together. Forget the risk. That Happy might go berserk and take it out on everybody on the newspaper staff didn't seem important anymore. Sam only wanted Marcy to be happy, too. She had a bad conscience about neglecting Marcy, but she thought she saw a way to make it up to her.

After Pip left, Sam began walking upstairs to her room, humming a little tune. She had supposed her parents were still engrossed in the wedding plans and was surprised when she realized her mother was following her up the stairs.

"Sam," her mother said. "I think we need to have a little talk about the dangers of premature emotional entanglements."

Sam groaned. "Oh, Mom, we've been all over that a hundred times. A thousand times."

"Yes, but I want to go over it again. Didn't you notice the look on Pip's face when you said you weren't going to get married until you were thirty? It was almost as if he were taking a personal interest. I must say I found it a little unnerving. After all most boys of Pip's age are not at all interested in weddings."

"Pip is not most boys, Mom. He is sensitive and caring and thoughtful. He's just—well, he's just wonderful."

"I am very fond of Pip," said her mother, "but I think, and your father thinks, that you are a little young to get so involved—"

"Oh, would you just leave me alone!" said Sam. She dashed into her room and closed the door behind her, leaning against it for good measure.

"Goodness!" her mother exclaimed outside the door, but after a moment Sam heard her walking away.

Sam felt warm with indignation. It did seem poor that her mother had to pick this particular moment of all moments to give that favorite speech of hers about premature entanglements. It was very insensitive. Here Sam was in the midst of planning something very delicate that would require just the right, very deft touch from Dr. Heartbreak, she was also woozy from lack of sleep and therefore not at her most robust, and most important, she was indescribably happy. Was this any time to rain on her parade?

Dear Dr. Heartbreak, she thought weakly, help!

Chapter Eight

"What does it matter what I wear to the dance if I'm just going to serve punch?" Marcy asked.

"But everybody will see you there," said Sam. "Who knows? This could be the night that destiny takes a hand in your affairs. This could be the very night that the boy of your dreams shows up and looks into your eyes—"

"Okay, Sam, if you are willing to lend it to me I'll wear it. I'll do my best not to get punch on it."

"Oh, don't worry about that. It's your color, Marce. It's definitely you." Sam laid the red dress out on her bed.

"What are you going to wear?"

"I'm going to get Mrs. Blitch to alter this blue one that used to be Robin's." Sam took it out of the closet.

"Oh, that's nice," said Marcy, fingering its skirt.

"Yep, it's been out of style so long it's actually coming back in," said Sam.

"So you'll be driving to the dance in Pip's Mercedes. I suppose he'll take you out to dinner at La Petite Marmite beforehand. It must be nice to be rich."

Sam knew it was no use telling Marcy that none of that mattered as much as she thought. Marcy had a blind spot about money because it was in such short supply at her house. To tell Marcy that being rich wasn't important was like talking to Luke about the value of obeying rules or to Pip about the stupidity of jealousy. Everybody had a blind spot, Sam thought, except for Dr. Heartbreak. Dr. Heartbreak saw all, understood all. When she thought about Dr. Heartbreak's plan to bring happiness into Marcy's life, she felt light-headed with excitement.

"I wonder if Luke ever asked Tanya to the Christmas dance," Marcy said.

"Tanya?" said Sam, turning to her in surprise. "Luke's not interested in Tanya."

"Tell her that. She's been dropping her books in front of him, tripping him, asking him questions about homework. If you want to get a look at the subtle technical points of a full-scale pursuit, just watch Tanya."

"She should possess her soul in patience," said Sam.

Marcy looked at her oddly. "You come out with the weirdest things lately, Sam."

"Well, she's wasting her time, anyway," Sam said, "because I heard Reggie asking Luke if he'd take the pictures at the dance. Reg wants to give his absolutely undivided attention to Yolanda Carr and Luke said he would do the pictures because he wasn't taking anybody."

"The pictures will probably be mostly of Luke's thumb in front of the lens. Reggie must be really gone on Yolanda to trust Luke with his camera," said Marcy.

Sam held the blue dress in front of her and took long graceful steps around the room watching herself out of the corner of her eye in the big mirror. "Yup, from what I heard I think 'gone' sums it up pretty well," she said.

"What were you doing? Sitting with a stethoscope pressed to the wall or something?"

The truth was, she had overheard the entire conversation while lurking at the water fountain waiting for Reggie to scram so she could stuff Luke's locker with Heartbreak letters. "Luke's locker is practically right next to mine, you know," Sam said, starting guiltily. "I just happened to overhear. They weren't making any secret of it."

"So Reggie's got this great passion now," sighed Marcy. "Everybody's got something going but me."

"Not Tracy, as far as I know," Sam said. "Not Anita, either."

"Thanks a lot, Sam. I really appreciate being classed with Anita."

"I just mean you're wrong about everybody being caught up in some romance, that's all. There are heaps of people who aren't going out with anybody. In fact, look at Luke. You know, I think you may have been right about him, Marce. He said something the other day that made me think he's gotten disillusioned with the whole girl-boy scene."

"I haven't even had a *chance* to get disillusioned," said Marcy. "Life has passed me by. I've been left at the starting gate."

Sam stroked the dress she had laid on the bed and smiled a little. "Maybe your luck is about to turn," she said.

"Maybe," said Marcy without much conviction.

The next day, Sam crept up to Luke's locker, spun the combination on the lock, pulled the door open and dumped a stack of letters in.

"Hi," said Anita.

"Good grief, you startled me," Sam said, slamming the locker shut. Where had Anita come from? Sam was sure she had checked carefully to see that the coast was clear. Anita must have grown up suddenly from a spore like a toadstool, that was the only explanation.

"What are you up to?"

"Nothing much," said Sam. "How about you?"

"Is that your locker?" asked Anita.

It was too bad that Luke's locker bore a sticker that said Help Stamp out Virginity. Sam didn't see how she could claim it for her own, even if it hadn't been for the smell of dirty gym shoes it gave off. Diversionary tactics were needed.

"Anita," she said, "have I ever told you how much I admired your article on the parole system? I thought it was clear, it was to the point, and most important it was written in vivid, muscular prose."

"You must have been the only person that read it," Anita said, her face darkening. "That was the one that came out the same day that Dr. Heartbreak column broke."

"Tell me," said Sam, edging away from the locker. "How do you get your ideas?"

"It's interesting you should ask me that. Kilroy has a cousin that's serving time for breaking and entering. So you might say he put me onto it."

"Amazing. And did you conduct person-to-person interviews?"

"Only with those who were out. The rest of them I had to do by letter. They don't let them have visitors over at the reform school."

"Fascinating," said Sam. "Are you thinking you'll do any more articles along that same line? Crime, I mean."

"Actually, what I'd really like to do next," said Anita, "is an exposé of that Heartbreak column. Can you give me any leads?"

The bell rang with a bone-shattering sound somewhere over Sam's head. Sam could feel Anita's gimlet eyes boring into her. "Gotta run," she said faintly. She fled to her homeroom.

Dear Sports Fan,
Your last letter touched my heart strangely. But if we are to meet, I must ask one thing of you—we must never speak of my being Dr. Heartbreak. When I tell you that I have broached my most sacred honor as an advice columnist to see you, I know you will respect my feelings about this. It must be as if we have never written to each other.

You must tell no one this, but *I am closer to you than you know*. I will be at the Lee High's Christmas dance in a red dress and with white carnations in my hair. Come up to me and say

"Carnations are my cat's favorite flower." Then I will know that it is you.

> Yours in Anticipation,
> Dr. Heartbreak

Dear Wistful,
Your last letter struck a soul-deep responsive chord within me, and I can no longer resist the temptation to see you and hear your voice. Beyond that, who can say what Fate may hold? I must tell you this—*I am closer to you than you dream.* I will be at Lee High's Christmas dance. Wear white carnations in your hair. I will say "Carnations are my cat's favorite flower." That will be the password by which you will know me. My little plum flower, I must make one request—we can never speak of my Heartbreak identity—

Sam bit her lip in concentration as she typed out the rest of Wistful's letter. "Et cetera, et cetera," she muttered. "That should do it," she said. She ripped the page out of the typewriter and sealed it up in an envelope.

She sat in the desk chair a moment heaving a sigh of satisfaction. To be sure, only a few months ago, she would not have figured that Jim Shipman was Marcy's type or vice versa, but as Dr. Heartbreak she was privileged the secret sides of their personalities. That was the tremendous advantage of being Dr. Heartbreak.

In the busy days that followed—fittings at Mrs. Blitch's house, wedding errands all over town, tons of reading for history class—Sam scarcely ever quit thinking about the upcoming Christmas dance and the drama that was to take place there. The very thought of it lent a special lift to her day. I'm like a fairy god-mother, she thought. I wave my magic wand and poof! Marcy's prince appears. As she mopped the kitchen floor, she sang, "Bibbity bobbity boo."

"I'm glad to see you're in a better mood lately, Sam," said her mother. "I was beginning to wonder if you resented the fuss over Robin's wedding."

"Oh, no. I want for everybody in the world to be happy," said Sam. "Robin and, well, everybody." She did a few dance steps with her mop as a partner.

"Have you given any more thought to what we were saying about premature emotional entanglements?" said her mother. "I know you think I'm being silly, Sam, but I just want you to keep in mind all the won-derful things you have ahead of you—college, a ca-reer, a chance to really make your own way. I wouldn't take anything for those years of my own life. Maybe it wasn't all easy, but look around you at the alterna-tive—the people who have jumped into parenthood and marriage and end up old before their time, di-vorced, burdened with heavy responsibilities."

"Mom," Sam protested, "all I said was I want everybody to be happy! Do we have to make a federal case out of this?"

"It was the way you said it that worries me, Sam."

"I'm not planning to get married, I promise. And Pip and I aren't doing anything we couldn't do on prime time. Why are you always on my case? Don't you think two heart-to-heart talks in one week is kind of pushing this communication stuff into the ground? I need space!"

Her mother frowned. "You seem so keyed up. Is anything on your mind?"

"Uh, no. What makes you think something is on my mind?"

The phone rang and Sam's mother reached for it absently. "This is she. Oh, hello, Mr. Schmidt. To tell you the truth, I was hoping to spend less than that. A good deal less."

Sam took that opportunity to quietly wring out the mop and tiptoe out of the room.

At the newspaper staff meeting the next day, Sam was glad to see that Luke reacted quickly to signs of Anita's interest in the workings of the Heartbreak column.

"Butt out, Anita," he said bluntly. "If you've got any questions about the Heartbreak column, bring them to me. Don't go nosing around talking to everybody else about it."

"All right," said Anita, her hands on her hips. "When those letters leave the post office box, where do they go next? That's my question."

Luke grinned. "I didn't say I would have the answer, but as a matter of fact, I have the idea Heartbreak sends a courier by to pick them up every now and then."

"It's easy enough to find out," said Anita. "We could just stake out the post office box."

"Now let me get this straight," said Luke. "You want to do an exposé of our most popular feature?"

"Why not?"

"Because it would destroy the feature, that's why not. Use your brain. Secrecy is fundamental to this column. Does David Copperfield start selling books on how to make the Empire State Building disappear for fun and profit? Does Spuds MacKenzie give out his home address? The fun is in the illusion."

"I don't believe in illusion," Anita said, pressing her lips together. "I believe in truth in packaging."

"Figures," Sam muttered, glancing at her shiny face.

"I think Luke has something," said Reggie. "If it ain't broke, don't fix it."

"You can't help wondering though, can you?" said Tracy softly. "I mean, wondering what he's like."

"He's obviously an intellectual," said Marcy. "Look at his vocabulary, his sentence construction."

"I think he's old-fashioned and kind of sweet. And, of course, very sympathetic," said Tracy.

"I think you're both wrong," said Danita. "The way I see it this fella is very hip, and the whole thing is just a big put-on."

"Oh, I don't think so," said Happy, staring thoughtfully at a thumbnail. "Anyone can sense the sincerity of his answers even if he may be a little thick skulled."

"There's some talk around the locker room that 'he' is a 'she,'" said Reggie.

"How do these rumors get started?" asked Marcy, disgusted. "Dr. Heartbreak, a girl? The idea is ridiculous."

"Listen to all the speculation, Luke," said Anita. "I rest my case. The people want to know who this Heartbreak is."

"Well, the people don't get to know," said Luke shortly. "If we bug Heartbreak he may just lift his column. Then where will we be? I want you to let this thing drop."

"Heil, Hitler," said Anita, saluting smartly.

But as she turned away Sam thought she heard her mutter something ominous about ways to skin a cat.

Minutes later, over by the supplies cabinet, Sam babbled out her fears to Luke.

"She's going to stake out the post office box, Luke," she said. "I can see it in those beady eyes. That girl is dangerous."

"How's she going to stake out the place around the clock? Now shut up about this, will you? What if somebody comes over here and hears us?"

"She'll probably get Kilroy to help her. And maybe some of Kilroy's criminal relatives. I'm going to be trailed by the alumni of Simmons Youth Center and Correctional Facility. I don't think I can take it, Luke."

"Get a grip, Sam. Anita's not the KGB, you know. She's got her homework to do just like everybody else. Now for pete's sake, shut up."

Sam, her eyes wide with anxiety, carried a stack of typing paper over to Danita. Luke might make light of her fears but he wasn't the one who would have to live with the consequences if Heartbreak were exposed. She decided she would not go to the post office at all this Friday. She had enough letters to see her through the next column. After Anita had sat out in the cold and the rain at the post office for over a week, surely her determination would begin to give way. With so much at stake Sam could not afford to take any chances.

That evening, Marcy called Sam in great excitement. "It's happened, Sam, it's happened. I've heard from Heartbreak and I'm actually going to meet him!"

"That's so exciting, Marce. Where?"

"At the Christmas dance. Can you believe it? You couldn't have been more right when you said that might be the night destiny came knocking. I am literally trembling so I can hardly hold the telephone. Do you think I did the right thing? You don't think I'm going to really regret this, do you? I've never done anything so wild before. I mean, talk about literally a blind date! I don't have the foggiest notion yet what he looks like and yet, somehow I *feel* sure I'll know him at once. Don't you think you can feel a kind of closeness with someone? I feel so silly still calling him Heartbreak, but I don't even know his name yet. Golly, this only shows how right I was to turn Chip down. Imagine meeting the love of your life with Chip in tow!"

Sam tried to concentrate on asking the right questions, the ones she would have asked if she didn't already know what was going to happen. "But Marcy, if you don't know what he looks like, how will you know when you meet him?"

"That's all worked out, Sam. We've got a code. Golly, I hope I don't get cold feet at the last minute. My fingers are sort of icy right now, just thinking about it. Do you think I can pull it off? I mean, it will be perfectly safe, won't it? I'm meeting him right in the middle of a crowded dance floor, what can possibly go wrong? Oh, Sam, I'm scared out of my mind."

"It's going to be just fine, Marcy. After all, if you do get cold feet you can just take the carnations out of your hair and go hide in the ladies' room."

"How did you know about the carnations?"

Sam swallowed. "Why, you told me just now."

"I did? I thought I didn't."

"You're so excited you don't know whether you're coming or going, Marce."

"It's true," sighed Marcy. "This is possibly the biggest evening of my entire life. I mean, nothing I have ever done has exactly prepared me for this. Tell me, Sam, are you surprised that I pulled it off? I mean, I thought we seemed sort of on the same wavelength, you know. He seemed so mature, so serious. But now I'm having this awful thought. Do you think he maybe goes around meeting girls all over the state? What is your honest opinion?"

"I think you'd better wait until you meet him to decide about all those things. You can just play it by ear."

"You're right. I know you're right. But tell me, if you were me would you be doing this?"

"Sure."

"I hope I'm doing the right thing. Golly, this is exciting."

At Fino's Pizza that same evening, Happy stared broodingly at her untouched pizza.

"Someone's been poisoning his mind against me, Lindy. He's started hinting around that maybe we should both of us see other people."

"Maybe he just thinks you both ought to be seeing other people. Maybe that's all there is to it."

"But why? That's what I keep asking myself. What's behind it? He used to be wild about me. He couldn't take his eyes off of me."

"Maybe he thought he was getting too serious."

"But we didn't have that kind of thing. It wasn't serious. Just fun, laughs, parties, good times. And honestly, I have been watching him like a hawk and he hasn't so much as looked at another girl, much less sneaked out behind my back. I have my sources, you know. I know these things. So, what can he *mean* that we ought to see other people? When *everyone* says we're the cutest couple around! I'm the best thing that ever happened to Jim Shipman. The best looking, the best dressed, the smartest girl he ever went out with. Where does he go from here but down, to be perfectly blunt? No, Lindy, there's only one answer and that is that somebody's been poisoning his mind against me. As a mere sophomore, you cannot be expected to know what evil lurks in the halls of Lee, but take it from me, there are those who would love to see Jim drop me, who would love to see me crying, embarrassed, heartbroken—''

Lindy patted her hand. ''Pull yourself together, Happy. It'll be all right.''

''It's probably Samantha Morrison or Marcy McNair,'' sniffled Happy. ''They would *love* to get back at me.''

''Get back at you for what?''

''Ancient history, little misunderstandings, and *so* unfair,'' Happy said disjointedly. ''It's too complicated to go into, but believe me, they have it in for me. Can you believe I actually *introduced* Jim to them. I was that stupid. But how could I know?''

''Naturally you don't expect people to go around talking about you behind your back to your boyfriend.''

''But when did they do it?'' cried Happy. ''That's what I can't figure out. Anonymous phone calls? Poison pen letters? Jim is at football practice every afternoon, and he's not the world's brightest, you know, so he simply has to slave over his homework.

Many is the evening I've spent over at his house helping him out when I could have been out having a good time. The *sacrifices* I've made! But does he care?"

"You're better off without him," said Lindy.

"No! No!" Happy wiped her eyes with a paper napkin.

"Have you thought about writing to Dr. Heartbreak?"

"Don't mention that fraud's name to me. I'd like to give him a piece of my mind. I did everything, but everything he suggested and what did it get me? His advice was so *totally* off the wall and so *hopelessly* ineffective that I honestly think his license or whatever should be revoked."

"So does this mean you aren't going to the Christmas dance with Jim? It's all over?"

Happy shuddered. "It's not as bad as that. Actually nothing is definite yet. He's just made these little feeble bleatings about freedom. Naturally I pretended not to understand him. I've already bought the most smashing dress—thin straps, bubble skirt. I'm not going to let him out of our date just because he says we ought to be thinking about seeing other people. I hope I have more gumption than that. Besides, he doesn't know his own mind. He seemed all confused about what he wanted to do about the dance. First he said he wanted to go. Then he said we ought to think this over. Then he said he didn't want to go alone, but I shouldn't think that if we go together it means anything."

"I see what you mean about him not being the world's brightest."

"He's confused by all that stuff they're telling him, that poison they're pouring into his mind," Happy sniffled. "Oh, I would dearly love to get my hands on whoever is doing this to me and make them pay, and I mean *pay*."

"You aren't going to eat your pizza, then?" asked Lindy, eyeing it hopefully.

"I hate that Sam Morrison," Happy went on. "I wish I could figure out what it was she wanted most of all in the entire world. Then I would take it away from her and sit there gloating. *That* would pay her back for the way she's taken Jim away from me."

"Maybe it wasn't her that did it. Maybe it was the other girl you mentioned."

"They're probably in it together," said Happy. "Those three are so tight you couldn't dynamite them apart. Marcy, Sam, and Luke—they've been that way since grade school. You can be sure that if one's in on it they're all in on it."

"You mean you think all three of them have been trying to get Jim away from you?"

"Why not? They hate me."

"But that's terrible!"

"It's a cold, cruel world out there, Lindy, take it from me." Happy blew her nose and Lindy took that opportunity to lift a little pepperoni off of her pizza to nibble on. Listening to the heartbroken was hungry work.

It was Marcy's turn to help Luke tie up the newspapers.

"Why do you do it every week, Luke? Why don't you let somebody else stand in for you for a change?" said Marcy, roping twine around a stack of the papers.

"I want to be sure it's done right, that's why."

"I'll bet Reggie could do it sometime and get somebody else to help him."

Luke smiled a little shamefacedly and thumped a handful of newspapers into a neat stack.

"You just like to do it, don't you? You get some kinky thrill out of it. Tell the truth."

"You got it. They're beautiful, aren't they, Marce? Look at them. Look at that gorgeous black type on the white. Feel the paper. Get a load of that masthead, the part where it says Editor-in-Chief—Luke Lancaster. I love it."

"You are a bona fide nut. That's what you are."

The two of them tied up papers in companionable silence for a while. Unlike Sam, Marcy didn't mind the monotony of tying up the papers. It made her a little late getting to her work but it was worth it to have this quiet time, watching Luke's long pale fingers tying twine. She liked to hear him breathing next to her, she even liked the faintly gamey smell of his sneakers. She was so lucky to have friends like Luke and Sam and yet, she thought, she was, in a way, still lonely. Especially now that Sam was going out with Pip all the time, she felt something was missing from her life. I need something more, she thought. I need something new and special to pick me up. She fell to humming as she thought of Dr. Heartbreak.

"You sound awfully happy," said Luke, shooting her a curious look.

"I am," she said.

"Something I ought to know about?"

"Do you believe in soul mates, Luke?"

"Geez, no!" he said, horrified. "Where'd you come up with a crazy idea like that?"

"Don't you believe that two people can have so much in common that they are just on the same wavelength somehow? They understand each other perfectly, you see. They are drawn one to the other."

"Boy, are you riding for a fall, Marce."

"You've just got a downbeat view of love because you only go after girls you're sure of, which means the ones that are totally gaga over your looks. Then when you get to know them you can't believe it that they're so awful."

"Now do I get to tear apart your private life, kiddo?" he asked, giving her a sidelong glance.

"Go ahead," said Marcy. "My life is an open book. Unfortunately."

"Oh, forget it. Good luck with him, that's all. You're going to need it."

Luke was surprised to find that tying up the newspapers wasn't giving him the lift it usually did. Even looking at the masthead didn't give him that old thrill. Funny how one minute you could be on top of the world and a little bit later everything seemed to have the juice sucked out of it. He thumped the last tied stack on the table.

"That's it," he said in a flat voice. "I guess we can go."

Chapter Nine

La Petite Marmite said the floodlit sign outside the gracious Victorian mansion with its spreading porches. The night had turned chilly, and Sam had to cope with her Aunt Margaret's evening cape, borrowed at the last minute. It kept trying to wrap itself around her feet as Pip helped her out of the car.

"We should be all right," Pip said as he scanned the cars parked along the curb. "It doesn't look very crowded tonight. I guess I should have made reservations, but I just didn't think of it."

When they went inside, the waiter took one look at Pip and put them at the best table near the fire. Pip smiled ironically at Sam. Being the Byron Tobacco heir was good for the best table in the restaurant, if nothing else.

Sam could feel the heat of the fire on her bare back, but she didn't really need the warmth of the fire. That was because she was warm with happiness, she thought. The fire sent a shower of moving light dancing through the crystal on the table. Pip had turned to watch the door, and she let her eyes linger on his profile. So this is love, she thought. This is what it is like to look at someone and catch your breath in surprise at the force of your feeling. She hadn't thought, somehow, that it would happen to her, not this way, when she was young. Her mother had been right. She was in the midst of a premature emotional entanglement.

"Look who just came in," murmured Pip. "No, don't turn around. Wait. They're coming in our direction."

To Sam's surprise, the bulky form of Anita Jolley sailed into her view. Anita was dressed in a black evening dress of dull satin that was cut to make the most of her very full bosom.

"Sophisticated getup," Pip commented.

Sam gazed at Anita in fascination. A dark-eyed boy was pulling out her chair for her at the dimly lit table in the corner. "That's Myron Roth with her, the chess genius," Sam whispered.

"For goodness' sake, don't stare at them, Sam."

"I can't believe how different she looks all dressed up," she whispered. "She looks like a fairly decent-looking, middle-aged woman."

"At least they can't hear us way over there. I don't think you have to whisper."

"Maybe they can read lips," Sam said, raising her napkin to cover her mouth. "Maybe I should talk about them like this."

Pip grinned. "I doubt if you have to do that. Besides, what else can you say? I mean, there is Anita. So what?"

"I just can't believe that Anita is here at Petite Marmite with a boy. It's incredible. And she didn't even write to Dr. Heartbreak!"

"Is that what she told you? Well, I don't see what's so surprising about that? Why on earth would you figure she would write to Dr. Heartbreak?"

"For help, of course!"

Pip smiled at her. "You don't think people can get along okay and manage their lives without Dr. Heartbreak's advice?"

"You'd be surprised at how many people write to Dr. Heartbreak," Sam said a trifle warmly. "And they find his advice very helpful, too."

"Well, actually." Pip tugged at his nose. She felt he was about to make a confession that he had written to Heartbreak, but just then the waiter appeared with the menus. Sam was just as glad. She didn't really want the jealousy issue to surface and pierce the pink glow of her happiness.

After the waiter left, Pip cleared his throat, having evidently thought better of his confession. "So who do you know who has written to Dr. Heartbreak?" he asked.

"Naturally I can't say if it's in confidence," said Sam, surveying the tall menu.

"Naturally not," agreed Pip.

Sam cast a surreptitious look over at the corner table. "I have to respect Anita," she said. "She did it her way—whatever way that is. I suppose he's attracted to her mind, don't you think?"

"Must be," said Pip, a smile tugging at the corners of his mouth. "That was what first attracted me to you, too."

"No kidding? Oh, don't tease me, Pip, stop it."

When the waiter appeared, Pip opted for steak and Sam for the *moules mariniere*. She might have just as well ordered a tall glass of water because it turned out she was too excited to eat.

"What time is it?" she asked a little later as she toyed restlessly with a mussel.

"Eight o'clock, why?"

"Don't you think we ought to be shoving off to the dance pretty soon?"

"And leave the rest of the steak? Not likely," said Pip, conveying a juicy forkful to his mouth.

"I just don't want to miss anything."

"What's to miss, Sam? It's the same stuff all evening—music, dancing, crummy punch. Did I say something wrong? You sort of jumped."

"Punch," she said. "Uh, Marcy's going to be serving punch, that's all."

"I don't quite see what's so exciting about that."

"Don't talk, Pip. It just slows you down. Eat."

Anita and Myron had ordered appetizers. Well, it stood to reason that Anita would be more interested in food than in dancing, thought Sam. She and Myron would be at that table half the evening. All right for them—they didn't have responsibilities the way Sam did. Not that she really thought anything could possibly go wrong but she just wanted to be there herself to see the thrilling denouement of her plans.

Pip was chewing a piece of steak and looking at her thoughtfully. "What's the big hurry to get to the dance?" he asked.

Sam swooshed a mussel around in its sauce, steadfastly looking down. "You know how I love to dance."

"So, next time we'll take a bag lunch," Pip said. She didn't like the intelligent look he was giving her. She was reminded of Pip's opinions about people meddling in other people's lives, opinions that had been firmly set in the days he was dealing with his dictatorial grandfather. She recalled, too, that she had solemnly promised him not to get involved in anything Luke thought up. She was beginning to feel uncomfortable about having so many secrets from him. She would have loved to confess everything. The only problem was Dr. Heartbreak wasn't just her secret. He was Luke's, too. It also occurred to her that she had no idea whether Pip had a temper or not. Perhaps it would be a good idea to test him on some smaller matter before coming out with a full-scale confession that she had done everything he most disliked and had most carefully warned her against.

A little later she noticed he was swallowing the last bit of steak.

"Ready?" she asked.

"I have to get the check," he pointed out. But when Pip lifted his eyebrows, the waiter rushed to their side and produced the check as if he had been waiting for this instant all his life. In a matter of minutes, Sam was gathering her evening cloak around her, and together they hurried out into the night air.

"Why do I have the feeling there is a script to this evening that I haven't had a chance to read?" Pip asked the streetlight.

"Come on," said Sam, hastily sweeping the cape into the car. "Let's go."

Pip got in on the driver's side and turned the Mercedes in the direction of Lee High. "Obviously something is going on. Aren't you going to tell me what? Don't you trust me?"

She thought fast. "Okay, but it's not my secret, so don't tell anybody. Marcy has set it up to meet her secret pen pal at the dance."

"Her secret pen pal? You mean she doesn't even know who this guy is?"

"Well, she *sort* of knows who he is. I mean they've been writing back and forth, but they've never actually met and she doesn't know his name."

"I get it. And she wants all her friends standing by to watch, right?"

"Not exactly. I mean, of course, I'm not going to stare at them or anything, if that's what you mean. But I would sort of like to see what happens, from a distance. That can't hurt, can it? Their very first meeting! Don't you think it's romantic?"

"No, I think it's crazy. But Marcy's not going to be taking my advice. Why didn't the guy tell her his name? It sounds pretty fishy to me."

Sam looked at him in astonishment. "Why, Pip Byron, how can you sit there and say that? You know you didn't tell me your name until we'd known each other for weeks. All that time I thought you were named Pip Winston.''

"Yeah, but I had a good reason for that. The crazy way people act in this town, practically bowing down at the name Byron, and heck, Sam, the way you were acting yourself, saying you wanted to go out with Philip Arrington Byron III when you didn't even know me.''

It was hard for Sam to even remember the days when the name Byron had called up vague romantic images in her mind. All of that was quite disconnected from the Pip she had gotten to know and care about. "All right, you had a good reason," she said. "But maybe Marcy's pen pal has a good reason, too."

"Well, I, for one, am not going to go over there and gawk at them.''

"Fine," said Sam. "Don't. But could you drive a little faster, maybe?''

At the dance in the Lee High gym, Marcy was a way ahead of herself with dipping out glasses of punch. She had all of twenty glasses lined up next to the bowl and filled with a rather revolting looking pink liquid. She was nothing if not efficient. But her hands were icy and they jerked spasmodically at the slightest noise.

Scanning the room, she saw Sam and Pip coming in. Whatever Marcy's own opinions about Pip, she had to admit his clothes were impeccable, and Sam looked so secure standing there, a slight blond figure, her arm resting in his, that Marcy's heart squeezed with a painful twinge of envy. Sam's life was easy. Sam didn't choke on her emotions the way Marcy did. She wasn't driven to spend long hours polishing her grade point average, feeling she had to either be on top or perish. And she wasn't forced, as Marcy was tonight, to stand waiting at the punch bowl, her cold fingers nervously fingering the carnations in her hair.

Marcy was beginning to regret she had ever agreed to meet Dr. Heartbreak. She wished especially that she had not told Sam about it. There was Sam now, smiling at her from across the room and giving her an encouraging wave. How embarrassing it was going to be if Heartbreak never showed up! And where was he, if he was coming? If he didn't show up it would only be typical of her luck, she thought.

Jim Shipman and Happy danced past her. A moment later she noticed that something odd was going on. Mike Valenti had cut in on Jim and Happy. Marcy had read, of course, of people cutting in on other people, and had seen it done in movies, but she had never known it to happen in the Lee High gym before, and she stared at the dancing couple, feeling vaguely surprised. At last Happy and Mike were lost in the crowd on the gym floor and disappeared from her view. It took Marcy a second after that to notice that Jim Shipman had come over to the punch bowl. Mechanically she held out a glass of punch to him. In spite of the turmoil in her mind, she was able to produce a weak smile.

"Carnations are my cat's favorite flowers," Jim said.

The punch cup slipped out of her hand as she stared at him, stunned. She scarcely noticed the two other punch glasses that went down like dominoes or the droplets of pink that sprayed her dress.

"Uh, what did you say?" she asked.

"I said carnations are my cat's favorite flowers."

"I thought that's what you said." Marcy swallowed as she looked up at him. Jim Shipman was Dr. Heartbreak? Jim Shipman's was the heart with which hers was beating in tune?

"I've been waiting for this for a long time," he said, striding around the table.

Before Marcy even took in what was happening, Jim's arms were holding her in a firm grip and he was passionately kissing her lips, her ears, her neck, while Marcy's eyes rolled wildly and she wondered where the chaperons were. This wasn't at all what she had expected. Had she been asked to predict what it would be like to have Jim Shipman kissing her, she never would have thought that she would find it repelling.

"Wait a minute," she said weakly. "I'm sure there's been some misunderstanding. I feel positive there has been a mistake."

She felt an uncertain tremor run through Jim's huge body. He pulled away and looked at her. "You are, uh, the girl I've been writing to, aren't you? I mean, white flowers, red dress, it all checks out."

"Well, yes, I *am* the girl you've been writing to, but—"

"All right, then," Jim growled in her ear. "Geez, you scared me for a second there. Now we know where we are. I've been thinking of you, dreaming of you, going crazy."

Marcy could feel his damp lips on her ear lobe. Yuck. She pushed against his chest with her hands, but it was like pushing against a truck.

"Jim," she said. "Let go of me. Let go of me."

He didn't seem to even hear her. She wondered if the noise of the band was drowning her out. It was as if she were wrestling with a gigantic octopus, and she suddenly felt weak with dismay. How could this possibly be Dr. Heartbreak? It was all some grotesque misunderstanding.

"Shipman, quit making a pest out of yourself," said a familiar male voice.

When Marcy saw Luke standing right behind Jim, she positively sagged in relief. Jim whirled around to face Luke, darkly flushing. "Mind your own business, shrimp," he growled.

"This *is* my business, Shipman. Buzz off. Can't you see Marcy's trying to get rid of you?"

"The lady and me were having a private conversation," said Jim, grabbing for Marcy's waist.

Marcy saw the color rise to Luke's face and to her utter astonishment his fist shot out and met Jim Shipman's chin. Shipman had overbalanced enough in his trying to grab Marcy that he was unable to save himself, and whether from the force of Luke's blow or from tripping over Marcy's foot, he fell back over all the punch glasses. There was a crash of glass as the punch bowl wobbled and fell. Dancers nearby screamed, but Luke, with great presence of mind, grabbed Marcy's hand and together they ran out of the gym.

They found themselves outside the gym in the cold night air, together listening to sounds of raised voices inside. The band had stopped playing, which seemed a bad sign.

"What do we do now?" Marcy whispered.

"We get the heck out of here. I don't want to be around when Shipman gets ready to deliver the second punch," said Luke. He grabbed Marcy's hand, and they bolted to Luke's car.

Sam did not even see Marcy and Luke leave. Event had piled on event too closely for that. When she and Pip had come in she had waved at Marcy and tried to beam encouragement in her direction. She was thrilled moments later when she saw Jim embrace Marcy. "Look!" she whispered, holding Pip's arm tightly. "They're kissing."

"Jim Shipman is Marcy's secret pen pal?" he said incredulously. "Jim Shipman?"

"Why not?" said Sam tartly. "He can write, can't he?"

"Just barely. I think she's trying to fight him off, Sam," said Pip. He was trying to see around some couples who had danced across their line of vision, blocking their view of the punch bowl.

"She's a little shy, I guess," said Sam anxiously.

Suddenly Happy appeared in front of Sam. Her black hair was perfectly coiffed, but her eyes were strangely wild. "You!" she shrieked at Sam. "You did this!"

Before Sam even had a chance to wonder how Happy had known what she had done, Happy slapped her. Sam reeled from the blow and held her hand to her stinging cheek. She was miserably conscious that everyone in the vicinity had stopped dancing to stare. Pip, who had wheeled around at the sound, saw the clear red mark of a hand on Sam's cheek.

Just then they heard a huge crashing sound on the other side of the room. "Fight!" someone yelled. "Shipman is down. Holy smoke, will you look at that!"

"You've always hated me!" Happy was blazing at Sam. "You sneaked him away from me. I'll get you for this!"

Pip was relieved to see that a chaperon was bearing down on them. A short blond girl and her date were tugging at Happy's skirt, trying to warn her.

"You poisoned his mind, that's what you did," Happy cried. "You told him all kinds of lies about me. I know it."

"She's real upset," the blond girl said to Sam earnestly. "She doesn't know what she's saying."

Pip looked at Happy's contorted features with amazement. If she had been a guy he would have known what to do, but an attack on Sam by a little bit of a girl in an evening dress confounded him.

"You've always hated me," Happy sobbed. Tears streaked her face, and her eyes were red.

"Sam, let's get out of here," muttered Pip.

But Sam only stood there, dazed. Pip looked around doubtfully, then scooped Sam up in his arms and headed for the door. His one feeling was that he wanted to put some distance between himself and all the craziness that had broken loose in the gym.

He could hear the chaperon's voice behind him saying, "We can't have this kind of thing."

The girl who had slapped Sam sputtered something but he did not catch the words.

"I don't care about any of that," the chaperon said. "You can't go around striking people. I want to see your student ID, please."

As Pip reached the open door, Sam, who had at first been limp in his arms, was beginning to struggle. "What's happening over there by the punch bowl?" she asked, trying to twist around to see. "Why has the band stopped playing?"

Once outside, he put her down and looked at her face closely in the light that fanned out from the open door. The mark of the hand on her cheek was slowly fading. "Who was that maniac in there, Sam? And what in the name of heaven is going on?"

"That's what I'm trying to find out!" Sam cried. "Did you see what happened to Marcy and Jim? We're missing everything."

"We didn't miss enough to suit me," said Pip. He cast a look over his shoulder. "People like that ought to be locked up, going around hitting people. Are you okay?"

Actually, Sam realized, she was shaking all over, and her knees were weak. It was very strange. She had noticed on television that people were continually striking other people, and they just bounced right up and went on to the next scene without so much as a Band-Aid or a frayed nerve to show for it. They were obviously made of stronger stuff than she was. She wondered if she was going to faint.

"You get in the car," Pip suggested, "and I'll go in and look for your cloak."

"Aunt Margaret's cloak," cried Sam. "I forgot about that." It was like Pip to remember the practical details even in the midst of confusion. When they reached the car, she let him tuck the skirt of her dress up clear of the door and lock her in. There was no use pretending she felt like heroics. Her knees seemed to have turned to Jell-O and the idea of having a locked car door between her and Happy seemed like an excellent one. She rolled down the window. "Pip, when you go in, try to find out what happened, okay?"

"I have this feeling you know more about what happened than I do," he said darkly.

"Just ask," she pleaded.

She watched him move toward the lighted door of the gym. He was silhouetted a moment against the light, then he disappeared inside. Sam sat in the car, hugging herself and shivering uncontrollably. It was cold and on top of it, she was frightened. Everything had been so perfectly planned. What could have gone wrong?

She was glad when at last Pip reappeared, tossed her cloak to her and got in the driver's side. "Okay," he said. "This is what happened as far as I can make out. Either there was a fight between Luke and Shipman or Luke hit Shipman for no good reason when he wasn't looking or, according to what one girl told me, Shipman was getting fresh and Marcy tripped him."

"Is that all you could find out? That doesn't even make sense."

"The one clear fact is that Shipman hit the punch table like a ton of bricks. I know that because I saw one of the chaperons putting a Band-Aid on his forehead, and his shirt was all spattered with punch."

"Gosh!" said Sam.

"Is that all you've got to say, Sam? Gosh?"

"Well, it didn't turn out quite like I expected," she gulped. "I have to admit that. What about Marcy and Luke? Did you see them?"

"They're gone," Pip said, casting his eyes out in the direction of Thirteenth Street. "Luke may have more sense than I gave him credit for."

As Luke's old Pontiac roared away from the gym down Thirteenth Street, Luke and Marcy at first sat in silence. Finally Luke said, "You want to tell me what was happening back there? Is Shipman the one that was going to be your soul mate?"

"I thought he was. But he's not. Oh, it was awful, Luke. He said, 'Carnations are my cat's favorite flower,' and then all of a sudden he was all over me."

Luke was looking at her aghast. "Sweet heaven, he must have a brain tumor or something. He really said 'Carnations are my cat's favorite flower'?"

"Luke, can Jim Shipman possibly be Dr. Heartbreak?"

"Shipman Dr. Heartbreak?" he snorted. "Don't make me laugh."

"But you see," Marcy blushed, "I've been writing to Dr. Heartbreak and we seemed to have so much in common that I arranged, well, to meet him and the password was 'Carnations are my cat's favorite flower.' Do you think—I know it sounds ridiculous, but do you think Jim could have gotten the password from Dr. Heartbreak and left him tied up somewhere?"

Luke looked at her with an expression she could not quite read but one in which astonishment played a large part. Finally he said in a choked voice, "I'll kill her with my bare hands, that's what I'll do."

"Kill her? Kill who?"

"Sam, that's who," he spat. "This had to be her crazy idea."

Marcy had not maintained a 98.04 average by being slow to grasp an idea. "Are you telling me Sam is Dr. Heartbreak?" she wailed. "That Sam planned this entire thing? That she gave the password to Jim Shipman and set me up to meet him?"

Luke's eyes were steadfastly on the traffic ahead and he said nothing, but Marcy felt she had her answer.

A sense of desolation broke over her, and she felt a tear making its way down her chin. "I feel so stupid," she said.

Luke looked at her briefly. "Hey, don't cry!" He clumsily fished a handkerchief out of his pocket and tossed it to her.

Marcy blotted her eyes. "It's just been such a shock. Such an awful experience. When I think of Jim back there it makes my flesh creep, and—can't you see what a horrible mess this is? You're bound to get expelled for punching Jim, and then it's goodbye to being editor. Mr. Perkins will have a fit when he finds out you've been in a fight."

"Maybe I'll skate by," he said. "Extenuating circumstances and all that."

"Happy will jump on this," Marcy sniffled. "This is her chance. Talk about a disaster!"

"Oh, I don't know."

"What do you mean, you don't know? I've been humiliated in front of the whole school. I'll never forget Jim pawing me like that right out in front of everybody, it was awful. And you're going to be expelled! I just know it!" She twisted the handkerchief frantically in her hands. "Honestly, Sam as Dr. Heartbreak! I can't believe it. It's just so incredible. All that time I was writing to him—it's unbelievable. I suppose she probably thought, in some distorted way, she was doing me a favor, but—how can you sit there *smiling* like that, Luke?"

"I don't know," he said. "I guess it's because I just had a sort of a nice surprise."

"It was amazing how he went down, I have to say," Marcy said with satisfaction. In the midst of her humiliation she could still take pleasure in the memory of Luke's fist connecting with Jim's jaw, if nothing else. Amid the dreadful events of the evening, that at least would remain a golden memory, Jim's huge body crashing down on the punch table.

"I wasn't talking about decking Shipman. I had in mind another kind of surprise," said Luke. He looked over at her. "Marce," he said, "do you think you could try me out as a soul mate?"

"You? Me?" Marcy asked blankly.

"What's so weird about that?" Luke turned the car sharply into the Burger King parking lot. The light from the big windows spilled out onto the car, faintly limning Luke's pale hair and casting a dull gleam on Marcy's red dress.

"No," she said suddenly. "There's nothing weird about that." She was looking at his eyes, those blue eyes. Of course, that was why she had known that her love would have blue eyes. Because it had been Luke all along.

"And so if I was to kiss you or something," he said, eyeing her cautiously, "you wouldn't go yech and feel slightly sick to your stomach or anything."

A giggle welled up inside her.

"Well, I can't kiss you if you're laughing," he said, aggrieved.

"Oh, yes, you can," she said.

"Well, all right." He drew her close and kissed her. "So how was that?" He looked at her anxiously.

"Nice," she breathed.

"You know when I saw Shipman over there with you, at first I couldn't believe my eyes. Something sort of snapped, you know. It hit me that I should be the one with my arms around you." He put his arm around her.

Marcy's last coherent thought before he kissed her again was that maybe she would forgive Sam after all.

"That's Luke's car!" Sam cried, pointing to the Burger King parking lot.

"By George, it is!" Pip said. He cut quickly across a lane of traffic and pulled into the parking lot, but to Sam's surprise he did not stop but drove slowly past the green Pontiac and went on instead behind the restaurant where he pulled up at the drive-in window.

"You missed it!" she said. "Didn't you see it? The big green Pontiac. I want to go back and ask him what happened."

"Oh, I know Luke's car all right, Sam. I ought to by now. But you can forget about me going back there. I might not know what happened at the dance, but I could see what was happening in that car. Luke and Marcy were making out." He rolled down the window. "Two medium fries and two Cokes," he said into the microphone.

"Marcy and Luke?" said Sam. "No! You must have it wrong."

"Want to go peek in their window?" he asked.

"But it's just not possible, Pip," Sam explained. "Marcy and Luke? No way."

"You don't have to act like it's incest, or something," he said. "Why *not* Marcy and Luke?"

"Well, it's just impossible, that's all. I mean, we're all friends. We've always been friends. That's all there is to it."

"Okay, Sam, I invite you to go back and tap on the window of that car and ask them what they're doing. Be my guest."

Sam swallowed. She remembered Pip's uncomfortable habit of being right. "It just seems very strange to me," she said.

"Stranger things have happened," he said. He pulled up to the window and a girl in a cap handed over a couple of paper bags.

Sam had eaten so little of the *moules mariniere* that she was actually hungry and when Pip handed her the fries, she began stuffing them in her mouth rapidly.

"Of course, now that I think of it," she said, swallowing a mouthful of fries, "Marcy never has been able to see Luke's faults. That's sort of odd on the face of it, don't you think?"

"Could be a clue," Pip admitted.

"In fact, when I think back on some of the things she's said..." Sam mused, chomping on another french fry.

"You can have mine, too, if you're that hungry," he said.

"Marcy and Luke!" Sam exclaimed. "It's just so strange."

"I find," said Pip, "that I kind of like the idea." It was no secret to him that neither Marcy nor Luke had much use for him. By and large, the feeling was mutual. Nothing would suit him better than Marcy and Luke developing a passion for being alone together. Not only would he be spared that awful feeling of being the odd one out when Sam cajoled him into going out with them, but he could presumably quit worrying about Luke's putting the moves on Sam. He hoped Luke and Marcy were crazy about each other. He hoped they got married and moved to Alaska.

"I don't think I like the way things keep changing," Sam said mournfully.

"That's the way it goes, though, Sam. You just have to get used to it. Now are you going to tell me what was going on back there at the gym?"

Sam thought about it a minute. She knew the Dr. Heartbreak column was as dead as a dodo, now. When Jim Shipman was pulled into the principal's office for fighting at a school function, he would probably talk his head off.

"You want the whole story?" she asked.

"I guess so. Something tells me I'm not going to like it, though."

She told him the whole story.

After she had finished, Pip sat for a minute with his hands covering his face. "Good grief, Sam," he said weakly. "Good expletive deleted grief."

"It's not my fault something went wrong," she said.

"So that girl back there was right. You really did sneak Shipman away from her with the idea of handing him over to Marcy."

"Not exactly," said Sam. "I mean technically I did. But he went off her long before I said anything, honest. He kept writing Dr. Heartbreak these letters complaining about her. He really did. I just gave things a little extra shove at the end."

"I suppose you realize that when it gets out that you were Dr. Heartbreak, the kids at Lee will be organizing a lynch mob and that girl will be leading the pack."

"You think it will get out?" Sam asked nervously. "I mean, after all, Jim may know he was set up, but he doesn't know I'm Heartbreak. And I don't see how Happy can really know anything, either. She had to be just guessing. Even Marcy doesn't know."

"So who does know?"

"Luke," she admitted in a faint voice.

"Oh, right! The pillar of the community, Luke. I forgot you said it was his idea to begin with. Well, you can't say I didn't warn you, Sam. I told you anything Luke cooked up would be bad news."

"It seemed to be going so well at first," Sam said wistfully. "I really got to where I liked it. It was fun finding out about everybody's secrets and it was nice sitting around listening to people talk about how sensitive Dr. Heartbreak was, and what an intellectual he was, with me knowing all the time it was me they were talking about. You aren't mad at me, then?"

"I'm just too floored to be mad, Sam. This is beyond mad. This is some major natural disaster, like a typhoon. You don't sit around being mad at a typhoon. It's a waste of time."

"I'm so glad you aren't mad at me," she sighed.

"Do you mean to tell me the only thing that worries you about what went on tonight is whether I am mad at you or not?"

"I can see there are one or two other little problems," she admitted. "Tell me the truth, Pip. Do you think I'm going to have to move to another town and change my name?"

He sighed. "I don't know. I guess we'll just have to wait and see."

Chapter Ten

Monday morning, a long parade of people were called one by one into the principal's office. Sam was one of the last to be called in. She had no idea what anybody else had said, but when her turn came, she told the whole truth and hoped for mercy. It was hard for her to tell what was on Mr. Hendley's mind while she was explaining the ins and outs of what had happened. Maddeningly noncommittal, he listened, pressing the tips of his fingers together, and looked very grave.

Unfortunately her interview with the principal was not by any means the end of her ordeal. After she left Mr. Hendley's office she was called in to see the school counselor and asked some searching questions about the quality of her home life. She had scarcely finished assuring the school counselor that all was well at home and had made her way back to algebra class when she and Luke were called in for a painful private interview with Mr. Perkins.

"I am at fault," Mr. Perkins began, which made Sam feel awful. She knew well enough whose fault it was. It was hers. "I have been very remiss," he went on, polishing his glasses vigorously with his handkerchief. "I realize now I should have stopped those private response letters the minute I saw them proposed. But the published letters I saw seemed so well-balanced, so harmless. Well, there's no use crying over spilt milk. Errors in judgment were made on all sides. I've talked to Mr. Hendley about this and he agrees that we should be grateful nothing worse occurred. Of course, this is the end of the Dr. Heartbreak column, I need not add."

"Of course," Sam murmured.

"The less publicity the better," Mr. Perkins continued. "Mr. Hendley pointed out to me a thing or two about possible school liability, which I found quite disturbing. I think a quiet cessation of the column is the best solution. Needless to say, violence of any kind cannot be tolerated and the perpetrators must be punished." He put his glasses on and glared at Luke. Sam flinched. Now it was going to come. Luke was going to be kicked off as editor, and Happy put in his place. Mr. Perkins looked down, doodled for a moment with his pen and then went on. "Luke and Happy will both have to serve three days in in-school suspension, beginning tomorrow."

"Happy?" exclaimed Sam.

"Well, she slugged you, didn't she?" Luke pointed out. "There were all kinds of witnesses. I've heard about it from six people already this morning."

"That's right, she did," said Sam in surprise. She never had thought she would be glad that Happy had slapped her in the face.

"I suppose Reggie can carry on with the paper for the rest of this week," said Mr. Perkins. "Reggie is very reliable." He shot a reproachful look at Sam and Luke as if he could have said a thing or two about the reliability of his other staff members. "Then I suppose we will carry on as usual, though there will be a certain awkwardness, naturally." He removed his glasses and began polishing them again. "I, of course, will be taking a closer hand in the day-to-day running of the paper," he said in a doleful voice. "I know I have made mistakes in the past. All we can hope to do in this case is to contain the damage. I am disappointed, very disappointed in you both, but I am also very much aware that I have failed to give you the guidance you obviously needed."

When Sam and Luke were finally allowed to leave Mr. Perkins, Sam had begun to feel a twinge of sympathy for Kilroy's relatives. Being a criminal was terribly depressing. After being lectured to all morning, it was all she could do to lift one foot and put it in front of the other. She wondered how she would have the strength to face her father and mother at supper. It went without saying that although her father had been tactfully absent from her interviews with the principal, the counselor, and Mr. Perkins, he would have heard all about everything and would have plenty to say about it. Luke's mother, who taught senior En-

glish, would have heard everything as well by now, but
not only was Luke notoriously indifferent to anything
his parents thought, but also Sam was aware that in
this particular episode, he was comparatively inno-
cent. She was the one who had caused all the trouble.

"This is awful," Sam said as she and Luke trudged
down the hall back to class.

"I don't know," said Luke irrepressibly. "I never
thought I'd have the privilege of participating in an
official cover-up. It's kind of interesting."

"I'm really sorry about your getting in-school suspension," Sam moaned. "I know it's all my fault. I
went too far. I got carried away. I was power mad. I
should be the one in suspension. You'll be in there
with all those criminal types, Luke. People who set
things on fire and carry knives to school and all. What
if something happens to you? I'll never forgive myself."

"Don't go all to pieces, Sam," Luke said. "We're
just talking about a few days and people don't usually come out of in-school suspension bleeding, you
know." He grinned. "Besides, my fame as the guy
who knocked Jim Shipman halfway to Christmas will
probably impress those guys."

"I wish I were dead," said Sam simply.

He slapped her on the back. "Come on, Sam, the
sun is shining, tomorrow's a new day, cheer up."

She looked at him incredulously, then she remembered about him and Marcy and found herself grow-
ing hot with embarrassment. For the first time she got
an inkling into how Luke and Marcy must have felt
when she took up with Pip. She had a funny kind of
left-out feeling, knowing that there was something

private between Marcy and Luke now that she wasn't a part of.

"Whoo boy," said Luke. "If we thought the newspaper staff was a little sticky before Dr. Heartbreak, we're going to love it now."

"Maybe I ought to explain to Happy just what happened. I mean, it really wasn't me that put Jim off her. Right from the start Jim was complaining about her. I can prove it. I have all his letters."

"Oh, come on, Sam. Do you think that's going to cheer her up any?"

"I guess not."

"From what I hear, Jim is keeping his mouth shut. His story is that he just got carried away for a minute and that he's deeply sorry for his ungentlemanly conduct."

Sam looked at Luke in surprise. "Why, he's embarrassed about falling for Dr. Heartbreak! That must be why he's not talking."

"That's not too surprising when you think of it, is it?"

"I guess not," she said slowly.

"I don't know how much Happy knows or how much she's guessed, but life goes on, Sam. Even after disasters. That's what you're going to find out. I ought to know. I've been in my share of messes."

Third period, Sam entered the staff room with trepidation. She discovered that even when she just looked across the room at Happy, her cheek tingled as if reminding her not to get any closer. Happy was sitting at a desk in the corner, her arms folded. She was wearing dark glasses, so Sam assumed her eyes must be swollen or that at the very least her mascara was smeared.

Luke had perched on the table in front of the classroom. "I guess you all know," he said, "that Happy and I will be out of commission for a few days, so Reggie will be taking over until Friday. Reg, did you ever find your camera? I sort of lost track of it Saturday night in all the excitement."

Reggie nodded. All the sophomores were looking up at Luke in open admiration, whether because of his coolness under fire or his victory over Jim Shipman, Sam could not be sure.

Marcy looked over and grinned at Sam, and Sam felt a rush of relief. Although she and Marcy had hashed everything out to the point of exhaustion over the phone on Sunday, and Marcy had generously assured Sam she bore her no grudge for what had happened, an entire morning of interrogation had left Sam in need of extra reassurance. She went over and took the desk next to Marcy's.

Reggie came up to the head of the class and began rather nervously reviewing the story assignments but Sam was not listening to him. She wrote in her spiral bound notebook, "How much does everybody know?"

Marcy reached over her arm and wrote, "Not much, but the rumors are wild."

Sam jumped at the sudden sound of Anita's voice behind her. "I've got a story all written up for you," Anita said. Sam saw her hand Reggie a sheet of paper. "You might call it a fast breaking development," Anita said.

"Violence Disrupts Xmas Dance?" Reggie read aloud. He looked at Anita in amazement.

Luke laughed.

"There were a few details I haven't been able to fill in yet," said Anita, "but I realized I could interview practically everybody who was involved right here during staff meeting so that was no problem."

"No comment," Luke said promptly.

"Anita—" began Mr. Perkins.

"Well, Luke's always saying he wants hard news," said Anita defiantly. "And here it is. Hard news."

Mr. Perkins took the sheet of paper from Reggie. "I think I'll edit this story myself, Reggie. Perhaps a few words about the disruption of the festivities would be in order as a warning to others about school policy on these matters, but we want to be careful to avoid anything at all sensational."

"Or informative, maybe?" Kilroy suggested with a sneer.

"On the *Cock and Bull* we told it like it was," grumbled Anita.

"Yes, well, this is a school newspaper, Anita, and we must be conscious of many considerations that do not apply to underground papers that have no official sanction," said Mr. Perkins. "This school will be here, God willing, when you people are all gone on to other things and it is my job and Mr. Hendley's job to consider the reputation of the school."

"Subject closed," murmured Luke.

To Happy, it had seemed as if the day would never end. First the dreadful interviews with the principal and the school counselor and then, worse, the stares and whispers that had followed her all day.

Tomorrow she would have to report to in-school suspension. She would be herded to a special lunch table where she would be forced to eat with the dregs, the very bottom of the barrel. It was a humiliation she would never, ever live down if she got to be a hundred.

But her crying and pleading had gotten her nowhere with Mr. Hendley. He had pointed out that he could hardly suspend a boy for hitting someone and fail to suspend a girl who had done the same thing.

The worst part was knowing that people pitied her. There was no chance now of her passing the loss of Jim off with a laugh. It had been awful when she had realized that Mike had only asked her to dance to get her out of Jim's way so Jim could make his moves on Marcy. And it had been a ghastly shock to see her own boyfriend in a fight over Marcy in front of everybody! But the very worst part, worse than any of that, was that she had shown how much she cared. She had exposed her vulnerability in a way no one would ever forget. After this, everyone would pity and despise her. Her life was ruined.

And the unfairness of it took her breath away. Luke had slugged Jim and he was a hero. But when she slapped Sam, it was a different story. So much for so-called equal rights.

When she came around the corner of the administration building, Happy saw Sam standing with Pip Byron in the parking lot. She stopped and stood in the shadow of the building watching them with a hatred so intense it made her eyes burn.

Happy had no doubt that Sam had engineered the entire thing. She had played the events of Saturday night over and over in her mind, and Sam's putting Jim up to it was the only thing that made sense. It stood to reason that Marcy had not been responsible for Jim's behavior because it couldn't have been plainer that she wasn't interested in him. It had to have been Sam who had set it up somehow.

When Happy thought back to the events of that horrible evening, she remembered seeing Sam come in a little late. Happy had wanted Sam to see her dancing with Mike in her beautiful new dress. But Sam had not even been aware of Happy and Mike as they had danced nearby. She had been looking with an odd intensity at the punch table across the room. And when the dance was over and Mike had disappeared, the reasons for Sam's interest in the punch table had become clear. Happy had seen it all then, had seen Sam's smile when Jim had put his arms around Marcy.

Oh, Sam was behind it all right. How she had managed it Happy was not sure, but it might not have been difficult. Jim was stupid and easily led. Somehow Sam must have given Jim the idea Marcy was crazy about him. You would have thought she would have checked that out with Marcy first, but nobody had ever credited Sam with brains.

Leaning against the administration building, Happy gazed at the parking lot as Pip bent to kiss the top of Sam's blond head. She then saw Sam reach up to touch Pip's cheek with a gesture of such tenderness that it came to her in a blinding flash what she could do to get back at Sam.

It wouldn't be easy, she thought, biting her lip. Pip Byron had seen her the other evening when she was, well, to be perfectly blunt about it, not exactly at her best. But she was sure she could manage it. She was no weakling like Samantha who was used to people taking care of her. She was a fighter. She had done difficult things before and she could do this.

She watched as Sam and Pip tossed their books in the back seat of the open car and climbed in. She was still watching malevolently as the white car backed out of its parking place, but Sam and Pip, their hands clasped over the gearshift, did not see Happy standing in the shadow of the administration building.

"I think Luke's right," Sam said, as Pip let go of her hand to wheel the car out of the parking lot. "Life goes on. I'll live it down. In some ways, it all worked out for the best, after all. Marcy and Luke seem awfully happy. And I really think there's a good chance it won't ever get around that I was Dr. Heartbreak. Mr. Perkins seems to want to hush the whole thing up and I hear Jim's not talking, either."

"You've got nine lives, Sam," said Pip. "Say, did your Mom and Dad ever make up their mind about those flowers or not?"

"Oh, my gosh, I forgot! The wedding! You know this wasn't exactly the best time for me to get in a heap of trouble at school. I'm going to *need* nine lives." Sam sighed. "And on top of it, I'm going to have to wear pink to the thing. I loathe pink."

"Don't worry. I'll be there to hold your hand through the whole grisly ordeal."

"I love you, Pip."

He grinned. "Now, don't go out on any limb. Don't say anything you're going to be sorry for."

"I'm not going to be sorry. I *love* you."

"You don't have to yell," he said. But as they sped down Thirteenth Street, he was smiling.

* * * * *

Does Happy get her revenge?
Find out in YOUR DAILY HOROSCOPE,
the next book
about The In Crowd.
Coming soon from Keepsake.

COMING NEXT MONTH
FROM
Keepsake

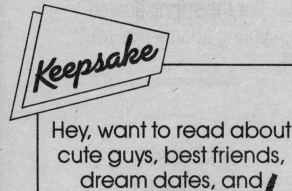